The Strange Story of
MARIA HALLETT

RICHARD ZAPF

This is a work of fiction. Names, characters, places, and incidents are products of the author's imagination or are used fictitiously and are not to be construed as real. Any resemblance to actual events, locations, organizations, or persons, living or dead, is entirely coincidental.

World Castle Publishing, LLC
Pensacola, Florida
Copyright © 2025 Richard Zapf
Paperback ISBN: 9798891264441
eBook ISBN: 9798891264458
First Edition World Castle Publishing, LLC, August 5, 2025
http://www.worldcastlepublishing.com

Cover: Cover Designs by Karen
Editor: Karen Fuller

Contents

CHAPTER ONE

I'm not crazy. At least, I don't think I am. Some would even say I'm too level-headed and a bit boring. How could I be anything but, after managing my own hardware store for thirty years? Being an old Cape Codder going back generations, I pay my taxes, keep up with my mortgage, love my wife and kids, and vote Independent. A few weeks ago, I came across a book in the Chatham Library. I read it, and then it was gone, and my wife and kids think I'm bonkers. I was in the mystery section of the library at the end of October, stocking up on reading material for the winter. There's very little happening on Cape Cod at that time of year unless you go down to the local pub and have a pint or two. I'll be the first to admit that I'm vulnerable to such outings, but I much prefer sitting in my chair by the fire with a good book while sipping a tumbler of single malt.

Among the books in the stacks with colorful bindings and flashy titles like *The G-String Murders* or *The Skeleton Valley Mystery* was a book that didn't seem to belong. It had an old leather binding with no title. Out of curiosity, I took it off the shelf, brought it to a table, and leafed through the thick parchment pages. It was a journal of sorts, written in an old eighteenth-century script. Making my way through the arcane language and unfamiliar script was a task too much for me, so I put it back on the shelf and went to the other side of the stack. When I came back with an armful of Robert B. Parker novels, it was on the table again. Strange, I thought, so I went to the front desk to inquire about this curious book.

The woman at the desk agreed to come back and take a look, stating, "Books that old are usually available only upon request, and only history scholars seem interested in them. If you want to view such material, you have to make an appointment. I'll be happy to take custody of the wayward book that seems to have escaped from the restricted stacks."

However, when we got to the table, I could find no sign of the book. I checked the stack, and it wasn't there. I panicked and looked up and down the stack with no result.

"Are you sure you saw the book?" she said.

"Yes, I can't imagine where it's gone. It was right here." I tapped the table where the book had been.

"Well, I've got to get back," she said in a bit of a huff. "Just bring it to the desk if you come across it."

I was never so embarrassed, and I was sure she thought I was nuts. Ha, I thought, the one place I didn't look was the floor. Down on my hands and knees, I scanned the floor and didn't find anything but dust bunnies. When I surfaced and looked on the table, there it was, open to the first page. *I've got you now, you little bastard*, I thought. I grabbed the book and decided to take it to the desk, but as soon as I picked it up, the pages became brittle and started to fall apart. The last thing I needed was to damage a valuable book, so I slammed the book shut and decided to leave the damn thing on the table. Let somebody else deal with this demon book. Then I packed to go and glanced back at the book, and couldn't believe my eyes. The damage had been repaired, and it was opened to the first page again!

This seemed more than a little

strange. I broke out in a sweat while the saliva started to dry in my mouth. But how dangerous could a book be? The eighteenth-century script danced before my eyes, and it was hard going at first. No author was credited with the writing. It simply started with these words: *There have been many stories about the wreck of the* Whydah *and the love story between the pirate "Black Sam" Bellamy and Maria Hallett. This is the only true account of their love and how the* Whydah *came to be wrecked.*

CHAPTER TWO

The story of the *Whydah* is well known on the Cape. In the 1980s, the wreck was discovered by Barry Clifford and his salvage team, and now there are two museums, one on the Cape and one in Salem, Massachusetts, chock full of artifacts from the wreck. I was hooked and wanted to read more. At that moment, the lights dimmed, indicating closing time, so I went to scoop up the book, but it began to disintegrate again, so I dropped it on the table. I couldn't believe I was about to talk to a book, but I did. "Okay, buster, I'll be back. I assume you'll be at your usual location," I said, and I walked out.

After leaving the library, I threw my armful of books in my car and headed across the street to the Irish pub. I liked the darkened room with its low ceiling. Irish memorabilia were packed in every corner, including travel posters and old mugs. It was a comfortable place to have a drink, and I figured I'd need at least three to collect myself and clear my mind so I could think rationally. Before I entered, I couldn't help noticing a 1960s vintage Chevelle Super Sport (SS) parked in front. It was all black, sporting Cragar Mags with Goodyear Wide Tread G/T tires mounted on them. Being a gearhead and owning a classic MG-TD myself, I couldn't resist taking a closer look. A peek under the rear end revealed there was a stainless-steel dual exhaust and traction bars to control the rear axle under hard acceleration. Inside were bucket seats and a Hurst shifter. In the back window, five "Over the Hundred Mile an Hour Club" decals from a drag strip that I didn't recognize were displayed. I guessed the driver must be inside the pub, and I hoped I'd have a chance to talk with him.

When I entered the pub, I was struck by the smell of the wood fireplace on the far side of the room. In addition to the usual decor were Halloween decorations. Witches and ghosts hung from the ceiling, and fake spiderwebs partly hid ghouls lurking in the corners. At the end of the bar sat a man dressed all in black with long black hair. It was hard to determine his age; he could have been between his late twenties to early forties. On the back of his jacket was the Chevrolet Bowtie logo. This had to be the guy with the Chevy SS, and I took the empty seat next to him. Riley, the owner and bartender, nodded and placed a tumbler of John Powers with ice on the side on the bar and said, "Your usual,

I presume, Joe." I introduced myself to the stranger, and after some small talk, I asked about the Chevy.

"Yeah, that's mine," he said, stirring his drink that had a swizzle stick with skull and crossbones on top. "To save you the trouble, she's got a 427 big block and six-pack carbs with progressive linkage. Passes anything but the gas station." He then paused and changed the subject. "Look at this place. An Irish pub, and they show no respect for Samhain."

"Come again?"

"It's a sacred holiday. At least, it was until the Christians got to it. They ruined it."

"So, are you a druid or something?" I asked.

He smiled, "No, I'm a lowly adjunct history professor at the community college, and I'm involved in the collection business as well. Pay sucks, but it keeps me in gas and whiskey. It's just that I'm not a Christian or a Jew, for that matter. I like to harken back to the old religion. It speaks to me."

I ordered another Powers. "So, enlighten me. Can I buy you a round?"

He nodded and continued, "Most people don't appreciate that this is a special time of the year."

"Really? It's coming up to Halloween, so it's special for my kids."

"Aye, it's the Celtic new year, Samhain, and the time when the curtain between the living and the dead is the thinnest. If you're lucky, you can communicate across the barrier. The old Celts believed that consuming booze helped make the connection. Of course, if you screw up, things can go badly for the dead and the living. But, you know, it's a time when people can patch up relationships and resolve long overdue debts. That sort of thing. But during the time of Samhain, you only have a small window to make things right between the living and the dead. These fools run about in stupid costumes and rot their kids' teeth with candy." He snapped the swizzle stick in half. "If you have business with the dead, now's the time to resolve it. Enough of this, I've got to get going."

"I didn't catch your name."

"Bartholomew Ryder, but Bart will do."

I heard the SS fire up, and from my seat at the bar, it sounded great. I could tell from the choppy rhythm of the idle that the engine had at least a half-race camshaft.

In the morning, I woke with quite a headache after drinking too much whiskey. My wife was not sympathetic. "What happened last night, Joe? Riley had to put you in a cab at closing time. Then you threw up all over the lawn. This isn't like you."

I withheld any reference to the book this time because I was sure she'd think I had really lost my mind. However, I was now on a mission, and every day after work, I spent time in the library. In a cubicle between the stacks, the book appeared open to where I left off the previous visit. As I read, I translated it from the eighteenth-century English:

Maria Hallett was a pretty lass, and as a child, she was thought of as a pixy by her older three sisters and four brothers. Always in motion, she loved to be outside. If there were chores to be done, Maria would be missing, running about on the dunes or playing in the marsh. Only her older sister, Liza, seemed to be able to corral Maria by staying one step ahead of her. "Maria's no mystery to me because I know her haunts on the dunes and in the marsh. After all, I showed them to her," she would say. When Liza caught up with her, Maria would readily comply and skip along beside her sister back to her chores, which she completed in a haphazard manner.

By the time Liza was eighteen, the dynamics in the family had changed. Their mother had passed away from a fever, and she had married Ben Jordan, a local smith. Maria had also changed. She was no longer a little pixy but a willowy fifteen-year-old redhead with blue eyes, and the male population of eligible bachelors began to notice her. Ezekiel Pratt, her schoolmaster, was smitten.

"Maria is like a wild filly, and to make her way through life, she'll need a firm but loving hand. I can provide that for her as well as a comfortable home life. I know she would make a good wife and mother in a year or two," said Mr. Pratt as he sat in Mr. Hallett's parlor.

"Well, she's young, and I'd be the first to admit that she can be headstrong and a bit wild, but if you want to court her, you're welcome to try," said Mr. Hallett.

"I'm sure once she's married and settles down, she'll see the advantages of our union, and a little tickle with the rod, I'm sure, will get her attention."

"If you think so, Mr. Pratt, but the rod hasn't done much to change her in the past."

When Maria was informed of the potential match, she made her feelings known. "No! I don't like Mr. Pratt. He hits us in school, and he doesn't smell good. Besides, he's old, and I am not ready. I'm determined not to get married until I'm much older, like Liza."

"Listen, Maria, you'll be sixteen

soon, and you won't be married until you're almost seventeen," said Mr. Hallett. "Since your mother died, I've been at wits' end marrying off your other sisters. At least Liza had sense enough to choose wisely and married a smith who makes a good living. Mr. Pratt has expressed his affection for you and can offer you a good life. Furthermore, he isn't seeking a dowry. You know he's richer than any schoolmaster has a right to be. When he comes courting, you will be civil to him, and maybe something will come of it."

Maria fiddled with the lace on her dress for a few moments and then said, "And if nothing comes of it, then what?"

Mr. Hallett paused. "Don't worry your young head, my dear, because something will come of it. There are no other options."

The day Mr. Pratt came courting,

Mr. Hallett made sure that Maria dressed in her Sunday best, a light blue dress that matched her eyes and a light blue ribbon woven into her hair. As Mr. Pratt walked up to the front door, Maria made an excuse to fetch her needlework and bolted out the back door. She ran down the street to the forge and found Liza.

"It's market day, and I'm walking to Chatham Center to do the week's shopping. Do you want to come along?" said Liza. Maria nodded. "My, you're looking fine today with ribbons in your hair and a clean dress. Is there a reason for that?"

Liza was the only person that Maria felt she could confide in, and said, "Papa gave permission for Mr. Pratt to court me. He's old, and he stinks, so I ran out the back door."

CHAPTER THREE

The girls spent most of the morning completing Liza's shopping list. Maria stood by the produce stall when three sailors came walking up the street. They were all big men and made a striking appearance with their sea boots, wide leather belts, ruffled shirts, and great coats. Two of them wore tricorn hats, but the biggest man in the middle had a wide-brimmed hat with a feather in it. None of them wore a powdered wig, although that was the fashion for officers when ashore. Even the girls could tell these were not average fishermen. They were bluewater sailors, and they looked like they had just arrived from some far-away port. They walked with a rolling gait, and their fine coats and hats indicated the sailors were ship's officers. Each tipped his hat to the girls as they passed. Maria locked eyes with the man with the wide-brimmed hat. His skin was tanned, and his hair was long, black, and braided into a tail going down his back, almost to his waist. She was struck by the blue eyes that glistened even in the shade of his hat.

Maria continued to watch the men as the two wearing tricorn hats went into the tavern while the man with the blue eyes remained outside, staring down at the harbor. "I'll be right back," she said and ran up the street before Liza could react.

"You seem interested in what's going on in the harbor," she said to the sailor.

"Aye, lassie, I've just shipped from England and am waiting for a ship coming from the Bahamas. I may be waiting for a while since we made a fast passage from England. It's unusual to have a following wind sailing west in these latitudes, but such a wind gave us a push. I could be waiting several weeks."

"What's your name?" she said, looking up at him.

"Sam, Sam Bellamy, and yours?"

"Maria Hallett. Nice to meet you, Captain Bellamy," she said as she extended her hand.

"Thank you for the promotion, Miss, but I'm not a captain yet. My new ship will be bound for a place called Florida and then the Bahamas. I'm to be her first mate. We have information about two Spanish galleons loaded with treasure that wrecked in shallow water. We plan to salvage them, and with my share of the treasure, I'll buy a ship, and then you can call me Captain.

"Well, in that case, Mr. Bellamy, if

you want to look for your ship coming into the sound, you need to walk on the other side of the hill where you can view the Atlantic and the ocean entrance to Chatham. If you have a glass, you can also see the rip channel beyond the end of Monomoy Island."

"I have no glass with me today, but I'll be sure to bring mine tomorrow. Perhaps you could be so kind as to show me where to stand and what landmarks I should look for, Miss."

A thrill went through her. Mr. Bellamy was young, handsome, and didn't smell bad. "How about noon? If there's any fog, it should burn off by then, and you might even be able to see Nantucket Island."

As they walked back to the market, Maria learned a great deal about Sam Bellamy. He left home at ten years old and joined the navy, after which he entered the merchant service and became a ship's officer. But the most important piece of information to Maria was that he said he had no special girl in other ports.

They arrived at the market, where Liza waited. As the girls turned to go, a horseman came galloping down the street and pulled the steed up next to them. Mr. Pratt dismounted, his face flushed with anger.

"Your father sent me to collect you," he said, grasping Maria by the arm as she cried in pain and tried to pull away. Sam reached out, grabbing Pratt by the wrist and squeezing until Pratt loosened his grip. Pratt grabbed a dagger from his belt with his left hand and raised it. Sam's right hand flashed out and caught Pratt by the wrist as he thrusted the dagger at Sam's chest.

Sam held both of Pratt's arms in a grip made strong from years of handling sheets, anchor rodes, and halyards. He pulled Pratt close until they were eye to eye, their faces inches apart. "I don't know who you are, but I can tell you're no fighting man. I've fought Spaniards, Moors, and Portagee, all men twice your strength. I suggest you reconsider your position." Sam then squeezed Pratt's wrist till the dagger fell to the ground. He pushed Pratt hard, so the schoolmaster stumbled and fell bottom first onto the street. Sam picked up Pratt's dagger and threw it at a tree ten feet away. It stuck point first and vibrated with the force of the throw. He then retrieved the dagger by snapping the point as he yanked it free, and he tossed it at Pratt's feet.

"I'm sure the ladies can find their own way home," he said.

"That woman is my betrothed," Pratt stammered as he mounted his horse. "You had no right to interfere."

Maria shouted back, "I'm not your betrothed and never will be!"

Sam tipped his hat and looked at Maria, "Until noon tomorrow." He then turned and went into the tavern.

CHAPTER FOUR

When Maria returned home, her father confronted her. "You're too old for the rod, not that it ever made an impression on you. So, I'll try reasoning, which didn't work with your mother or your sisters, for that matter. Don't you understand that Mr. Pratt is an excellent match? He's rich and well respected in the community. You'll have a fine house and servants, and by running out today, you insulted him."

"No, I won't. I hate him."

"Well, I guess the only solution is to confine you to your room until you come to your senses."

Mr. Hallett pushed Maria into her room. She sat on the bed and started to cry as she heard the key turn in the lock. Trapped on the second floor, she was desperate to see the handsome Sam Bellamy, who had rescued her from the clutches of the odorous Mr. Pratt. Sunrise came, and she woke up still dressed and feeling more hopeful because she had a plan that came to her in a dream. She'd climb out of the window and use the wisteria vine growing up the side of the house to climb to the ground. She'd done it before when she was little, but now Maria weighed twice as much. Taking a risk, she threw her coat and shoes out of the window and scampered down the vine. It turned out her anxiety over the vine failing was misplaced.

She wrapped herself in her cloak as she shivered, stepping on the road covered with an early morning frost, but this mattered little because she anticipated seeing Mr. Bellamy. The sound of a horse coming from behind startled her. First, she thought that it might be Pratt. When she turned, she saw a rider dressed in black mounted upon a black stallion with a saddle, bridle, and stirrups trimmed in silver. There was a silver-hilted sword with its scabbard lashed to the saddle, and on each side of the pommel were holsters holding silver-handled pistols. Her eyes bulged, and she took three steps back.

As he pulled up next to Maria, her heart pounded. She could see only part of his face since his eyes were shaded by the brim of his hat. The stranger touched the brim of his hat with his gloved hand. "Good morning, Miss. You're out early. May I ask where you're bound?"

Maria's jaw dropped, and she immediately became suspicious, "Are you a highwayman?"

"Oh no, lassie. Some say I make an honest living, but you haven't said where you're bound," he said, leaning forward in the saddle.

"Chatham Center. I'm to meet a friend."

"Excellent. If you like, I can give you a lift," he said as he extended his hand.

She took a step back. Maria had been filled with many tales of young women being stolen or murdered under such circumstances. "Thank you for the kind offer, but I prefer to walk."

"In that case, I hope you don't mind if I walk with you. I've been on a long journey and had no company, especially not someone as pretty as you," he said, dismounting. The horse threw back his head, and the stranger reached out to calm the animal. "Steady, Diablo." He patted the horse's neck.

"Doesn't that mean *devil* in Spanish?" she asked.

"Well, he can be the devil sometimes, hence the name."

"So, you said some say you make an honest living, so what do you do?"

"Aha, I solve problems for people when they're on a lee shore, as a sailor would say. For instance, I'm solving a problem for you right now free of charge."

"Really?"

"Of course. Seeing you on the road shortly after sunrise made me think that you're on a mission and may need protection. You never know when robbers or brigands might come out of nowhere. Now, as a gentleman, I'm obligated to see you safely to Chatham."

"You said you would help me for free," she said in a suspicious tone, "but that suggests that you charge for your services."

"You might say that," he said with

a smile that didn't quite reach his eyes.

"You mount a fine horse, so you must charge a big fee."

"Excellent observation. First, you should know that once I enter into a contract, I deliver what is required as long as the party to the contract holds up their end."

"Well, I don't know your name, but it seems, looking at Diablo and how you're armed, that you're probably good at collecting from those who refuse to pay."

"Precisely, my dear, and my name is Bartholomew Ryder."

As they walked to Chatham, Maria became a bit more comfortable with Mr. Ryder. They crested the hill where she planned to meet Sam. She could recognize him at fifty yards. He wore a fine red coat with silver buttons, faun britches, and the same hat. A cutlass hung from his belt.

"I can see why you were so anxious to get to Chatham. Good luck with your sailor, lassie. Now, I've other business to attend to. Perhaps we'll meet again," Mr. Ryder mounted Diablo, tipped his hat, and rode away.

"You're wearing a cutlass, Mr. Bellamy. May I ask why?" said Maria as she approached the sailor.

"Aye, miss, after yesterday, I was advised by my mates that I may need it to repel boarders," he said as he patted the hilt of the cutlass.

"It was very brave of you, and I thank you for what you did yesterday. I have never liked Mr. Pratt. The way that he looks at me gives me the chills, and he has a foul odor about him." She shivered slightly and looked up into his eyes, which seemed filled with compassion.

"Yes, I thought I caught a whiff of him that was quite disagreeable yesterday." Then Sam laughed. "When you got home, were you punished?"

"Not severely. My father knows it's no use to give me the rod. He tried to reason with me and locked me in my room, but I escaped this morning by climbing out the window. Then I met the oddest man riding a black horse he called Diablo, and he escorted me to town. Perhaps you saw him."

"I'd love to meet such a man that would deliver you to me, but I confess I was so excited to see you again that I searched with my glass. I saw you at quite a distance. You seemed to be skipping along, talking to yourself. I hope you were saying kind things about me, but I saw no one with you."

"Perhaps you were mistaken, and your glass was not properly adjusted?"

"Miss Hallett, I've been a sailor since I was ten. At twenty-three and a ship's officer, I know how to adjust a glass, and I saw no one."

"Let us not be disagreeable. We'll search for ships instead," she said.

Sam started to put events together. He said, "To arrive here at noon, you must have escaped early. Have you eaten?"

"No, Mr. Bellamy, I had nothing to eat last night or this morning since I was locked in my room." Her stomach grumbled. Maria giggled, hoping Sam didn't notice.

Sam smiled and pretended he didn't hear. "Then, Miss Hallett, I'll have the tavern keeper's wife make us a basket, and we'll have what the French call a picnic. We'll take our repast to the dunes, from where we can watch the ships go up and down the sound. I have to confess that after meeting you, I hope my ship takes its time arriving at Falmouth."

This was more than Maria expected. She spun in a circle, and her dress billowing out seemed to express her inner joy. "I'm starved, and I know just the place to go, where some high dunes overlook the sound."

Sam went into the tavern to fetch a basket containing bread, cheese, wine, and some of last night's chicken. During his absence, Maria looked down the street, and she saw Pratt walking with a determined gait toward her. He scowled, and as he got within arm's length, he said, "There you are. You're to come with me immediately. Your father has ordered it so."

Maria panicked. She turned to run into the tavern and fetch Sam, which was the only way she could escape being dragged home, and Pratt looked angry enough that she thought he might beat her. At that moment, Sam came through the tavern door, and they bumped into each other. He stared at Pratt and handed the basket to Maria while he slowly moved his hand to the hilt of his cutlass. Pratt stopped and backed away. Maria put her arm through Sam's and leaned into him as Pratt gasped. His eyes were wide, and his open jaw almost sagged to his knees. Sam made a step toward him, and Pratt turned and ran. Maria put her hand over her mouth and laughed.

As they picnicked in the dunes, she hung on every word while Sam told her about his adventures at sea. At the same time, Sam listened as Maria described her family life, and until her mother's passing, it sounded appealing.

Maria didn't go home for the next week but stayed at Liza's cottage. She saw Sam every day. On the sixth day, walking the dunes, he took her hand and kissed her. It wasn't their first kiss, but to

Maria, it felt special.

Sam looked at her. His eyes appeared soft, not hard, and focused like he was searching for a ship on a distant horizon. "I'm taking you back to your father and asking for your hand," he said. "If you'll have me?"

Maria knew they were growing close, and she had secretly hoped for a proposal that seemed like a ship still over the horizon. But now that ship sat unexpectedly tied to the quay. She faced him, entwining her fingers in his shirt so she could balance while standing on her toes, and kissed him.

CHAPTER FIVE

When Sam requested an interview, Mr. Hallett was surprised and intimidated by Sam's size and the cutlass hanging by his side. With some trepidation, he granted it, and a sense of relief swept over him when Sam left his cutlass in Maria's custody as she waited on the porch. Mr. Hallett said, "I cannot sanction you taking my daughter's hand. You're a penniless sailor with no prospects. You think you can make your fortune salvaging treasure? It's a joke, and you have no doubt made the same promise to a gullible lass in every port you've ever been to. Everyone knows sailors can't keep their word."

Sam's face became red. He leaned forward in his chair and said, "Sir, let me assure you that what you are saying doesn't apply to me. I'm a ship's officer, and I'll make my fortune. When I do, I'll come back and have Maria's hand. She says there's no other for her, and the same goes for me."

"On the contrary," said Hallett with a smirk, "she is betrothed to Mr. Pratt, and I'll have the announcement made in church within the months' time. Good day, Mr. Bellamy."

Sam looked Mr. Hallett in the eye and held his gaze, saying, "Mr. Hallett, let me leave you with this thought: if I were to die this instant, Maria would still not have Mr. Pratt. She does not love him."

Sam's attempt to gain Maria's hand had failed, and worse, she was now at home under close supervision. Maria managed a moment alone before he left. He kissed her cheek, which was wet with tears. "What happens to us now?" she asked.

He gripped the hilt on the cutlass and drew it a quarter way out of the scabbard, then slammed it back into place. "Be assured, I love only you, and you will be my bride. It may take time to change your father's mind, but you will be mine."

At home, Maria resumed enduring visits from Mr. Pratt, who droned on, repeating how lucky she was to have him as a suitor. She pulled away at any attempt he made to touch her and wouldn't look at or speak to him. Finally, he said, "You'll see. Once we're married, you'll be more compliant." He slapped his riding crop against his leg.

Several weeks went by until Maria got a visit from Liza. "Mr. Bellamy came to my cottage yesterday," the older sister reported, "and his ship has arrived. Once it's provisioned, he'll have to leave, but he wants to see you before he departs. He said he'd meet you on the dunes. You know the place. He'll be there every night until he has to leave."

"How can I see him? Papa watches my every move, and as you can see, they've put me in a different room upstairs. I'm locked in until I come to my senses and agree to marry Mr. Pratt. This Sunday, Papa is going to have the banns read in church. They'll have to drag me down the aisle, and I'll refuse to say 'I do.'"

Liza smiled. "When the lights go out tonight, Ben will be watching, and he'll put a ladder up to your window."

Maria smiled to herself and felt excited for the first time since she'd been locked up. She had a plan that, in her teenage brain, would guarantee Sam would be true to her and also drive away

Mr. Pratt.

Maria had no trouble navigating the dunes in the darkness. At first, she panicked when she didn't see Sam. She clenched her fists in frustration, but then she heard his voice whisper, "Maria, is that you?"

She smiled and replied, "Who else would it be? One of your strumpets from another port?"

She felt a hand grasp her ankle and pull her leg from under her. She was upended, landing on Sam. They embraced, and for the first time, she gave herself to him. They lay together until sunrise. Maria nestled in his arms. She had never felt so content and protected in her life, and she wanted to stay in his embrace forever. He pulled her close. "It's time to leave," he said.

"No, stay! We can run away, and I could go to sea with you. I climbed the wisteria vine to get to the ground. I bet I could climb the rigging."

"I bet you can. I would take you with me, but sailors think that it's bad luck to have a woman aboard. If I were captain, it would be different. I'll return in a year or two, three at the most, and shower you with riches. You'll have a fine house, and you'll be a captain's wife. How many children would you like?"

Her eyes filled with tears, and she clung to Sam as he pulled her closer, but she knew that Sam was right. She'd have to wait, and she hoped the first part of her plan was already working.

CHAPTER SIX

As I read through the book and came across Bartholomew Ryder, I wondered if he might be the same guy I had met at Riley's. No, that would be impossible and crazy—but wait, so is a magic book that can fix itself. If I asked Bart straight out, he'd probably laugh in my face. I knew I'd need a John Powers or three to think this problem through. Weeks ago, I thought selling supplies to contractors was complicated, but dealing with the book and Bart was on a different level.

Perusing the book, I came upon several chapters that dealt with the history of Sam Bellamy, who became known as "Black Sam" Bellamy. In consulting other books and visiting a museum nearby on Cape Cod, I found that he was a failure when it came to finding a wrecked treasure galleon. As a result, he and the rest of the treasure seeking crew decided to "go a-pirating."

During the early stages of his career, he rubbed shoulders with the likes of Edward Teach, better known as Blackbeard, but they soon parted ways. Bellamy was elected captain of his own ship and raided throughout the Caribbean. He and his crew captured over fifty vessels and amassed a fortune, with the biggest prize being the *Whydah*. She was a large, fast slave ship filled with treasure from selling off her cargo. Bellamy made her the flagship of his fleet of five pirate vessels. The *Whydah* carried over thirty guns, and with her, he commanded the most powerful fleet in the Caribbean. Much of his success resulted from his considerate treatment of his captives, whom he usually released unharmed and returned their ship minus any valuables. He was called the Robin Hood of pirates, but there is no record that he ever gave to the poor.

Bellamy also recruited sailors from the ships he captured. Most signed voluntarily, but sometimes, he came across specialists that he needed to run his ships, like sailmakers, carpenters, or gunners. Bellamy put pressure on these men to volunteer. He had his second-in-command show the prospective recruit a loaded pistol and a human skull with a bullet hole in it next to the ship's register. Most prospects got the message and signed.

Why the fleet broke up isn't clear. Some of the crew may have wanted greater independence, but other sources suggest that Bellamy was finished with the pirate life and still pined away for his love, Maria Hallett.

What is certain is that the *Whydah*, while in the company of another vessel, continued to plunder the east coast of the colonies until, caught in a gale off Cape Cod, she wrecked on the sand bars off Wellfleet. Many historians judged Bellamy to be an excellent seaman, so deception may have caused the wreck, along with his impatience to reunite with Maria. All but three of the crew were assumed drowned. But there may have been other survivors since the *Whydah* struck the shoals at night, and the Cape Codders were more interested in salvage than looking for survivors.

As I paged through the book, I continued to be curious about its construction. It was written on parchment in a brown ink, which seemed odd to me. I was advised by those who know better than me that iron oxide in the ink used at the time caused the brown color. I accepted this explanation until I happened to sustain a papercut while turning one of the pages. My finger bled enough that a few drops fell on the page. After wrapping a tissue around my finger, I wiped the blood from the page. A few minutes later, a chill went through me as I observed my dried blood looked the same color as the ink! This led me to the conclusion that the book may have been written in blood. I was tempted to snip part of a page with some script on it, but the damn book had outsmarted me before. I knew it wouldn't be willing to part with any of its pages, no matter how small. I had a blotter with me because, being old-fashioned, I like to write with a fountain pen. I also had a bottle of water, so I moistened the blotter and pressed it on the page, taking up the ink and my drops of blood from the page. I have a friend who works dating manuscripts in an archeology lab at a university in Boston and who owes me a few favors. I had given him a deal on all the plumbing fixtures when he renovated his antique house. I figured it was time for payback, and he'd be able to determine the makeup of the ink.

CHAPTER SEVEN

Maria continued to endure visits from Mr. Pratt, but now that Sam promised to return, she had the strength to wait. Any of Pratt's continued attempts to engage her resulted in a scornful look and Maria turning away. Liza's visits finally exposed Maria's plan. They sat in Maria's room as Liza opened a basket. "I've got some fresh apples and fried chicken. You've been looking pale, and I know you love fried chicken, so this should put some color in your cheeks."

"I'd rather not. I've not been feeling well. You can leave it, and maybe I'll have some later."

"Yes, you've not been feeling well since Sam went to sea, and I fear that your illness is more than being lovesick, dear sister."

"No, it's not," said Maria, jutting out her jaw.

"You forget that I've had two of my own, so I know the symptoms well. Besides, it's been three months since Sam has gone, and you've always been a skinny little thing, and your belly is sticking out. You're with child, and you won't be able to hide it for long. I hope Father steps forward to protect you, or you'll be called before the town fathers and punished."

"I don't care. Sam will come back, and we'll go away together."

Liza agreed to keep her secret, but her prediction was accurate. Within the week, the bulge of the babe growing in Maria's belly became apparent. Mr. Hallett called a midwife to confirm the pregnancy. After the midwife left, he stormed into Maria's room and threw her on the floor.

"You little whore! You've ruined everything. I gave you the opportunity to have a good life and a position of respect in the town, but instead, you open your legs for a penniless sailor who you barely know." He punctuated each phrase with a blow from a riding crop. She squeezed her eyes shut to force back the tears, rolling on her side to take his blows on her arms and back, protecting her belly and the babe. "You stupid girl. You've sinned, and you're no longer a daughter of mine." He dragged her by her hair down the stairs. "Mr. Pratt will now have nothing to do with you, and I disown you. You can take that offspring from the devil with you!" He opened the door and threw Maria out into the street, followed by a small bundle of her clothes.

Maria lay in the street and didn't move for some time. She cried, deeply hurt by her father's reaction. On the other hand, she felt relieved that she'd see no more of Mr. Pratt. As darkness closed in, Maria realized she had no place to find shelter. The weather was mild for October, so she decided she'd sleep in the dunes where she'd eventually perish along with her unborn child. As she started to get up, she heard the sound of a horse. Bartholomew Ryder tipped his hat, "You seem to be having a bad day, Miss. Can I be of service?"

"Perhaps, Mr. Ryder, but I have nothing, so I fear that I couldn't afford your fee."

"Fear not. When people sign with me, they usually pledge some sort of future payment or service. Some have lived in my debt for a considerable time before they found a means to make payment. Sometimes I write a contract stating 'to be paid with unspecified goods or services at a later date.'"

"Thank you, Mr. Ryder, but I don't wish to be in debt to anybody. I'll make my own way."

"Suit yourself, Miss. Just remember, I have appointments and obligations here about for the next few days, and then the offer is likely to expire." As Mr. Ryder galloped off, Maria looked down at the street and saw that Diablo had left no discernible hoof prints. *Maybe I can't see them because it's dark*, she thought.

The next day, Liza confronted her father. "You disowned your daughter who loves you. How cruel can you be?"

"She sinned, and she's no daughter of mine. She carries the seed of that devil Sam Bellamy."

Liza never thought she'd speak to her father in a disrespectful way, but she blurted out, "Fathers love and protect their children. You're an ogre. Mean with no feeling. You leave a young woman carrying your grandchild with no way to fend for herself."

"She can fend for herself the way she opened herself for that sailor."

Liza's eyes grew wide, and her whole body trembled, "You lost one daughter last night, and now you've lost another today." She slammed the door and headed for the dunes in search of her sister.

Liza found Maria huddled in the dunes. "Come with me," she said.

"No, Liza. I'd rather die where I lie," said Maria as she curled in a ball, covering her head with the small bundle of clothes.

"You're not going to die. You're coming home with me, where you can be safe. You can help me with my young ones and bide your time until Mr. Bellamy comes to fetch you." If he ever comes to fetch you, thought Liza.

Liza's promise of safety lasted three days, when the sheriff came to arrest Maria, clapping her in irons. On October 31, she was placed in the dock and accused of moral indecency.

It came as no surprise that her major accuser was Mr. Pratt.

"This woman has no moral fiber," he stated in the trial. "Even in school, she was unruly, and as a young woman, she has cavorted with the worst elements of society. She even planned with one of them, Sam Bellamy, to attack me."

"You were the first to draw a dagger!" Maria shouted from the box.

"She lies," said Pratt, "and she lay with that sailor, and now she carries his child, breaking her betrothal to me."

"I'd never marry you. You're old and smell like a soil pit, and the tip of your dagger is broken."

Even though the assembled crowd laughed, he continued, "See how defiant and ungrateful she is. Even her father has cast her out. She needs to be whipped, exiled, and kept away from decent people for the rest of her life."

The sentence was read out. "Maria Hallett, you are found guilty of immoral and indecent behavior and will receive a dozen lashes and be exiled from The Town of Chatham for the rest of your life. Let no one in the community give Maria Hallett aid or succor."

She looked across the assembly. None of her brothers and sisters were there except Ben and Liza, who sat with tears running down her cheeks. However, in the back of the assembly, standing in the darkest corner, was Mr. Ryder. The sheriff immediately took her to the whipping post, where his deputy hoisted her by her wrists until her toes hardly touched the ground, so she looked like a freshly caught cod dangling from a fishing line. As they laid her back bare, the drunken Sutton twins hoped to see more than her back. Both of them had been whipped for petty thievery and public intoxication, and they relished seeing someone else feel the sting of the cat.

In the flickering torchlight, the sheriff laid on the first stroke, raising welts on her back. She stiffened but didn't cry out. The second lash broke the skin, and Maria still didn't cry out, but Liza did and ran to the post, placing herself between Maria and the sheriff.

"Enough!" she shouted. "This woman is with child. If you harm Maria, it makes you hateful, despicable, self-righteous hypocrites, but if she dies or miscarries, and an innocent child dies with her, that makes you all guilty of murder and the worst sinners of all."

The sheriff reached forward to pull Liza away, but from under her cloak, she brandished a dagger. "This is made of the finest steel my husband can forge. It's your decision if you want to wear it as a decoration in your chest." She curled her body like a snake that was ready to strike. "If exile is your decision, that is one thing, but murder is a sin." She turned and, with one swipe of the blade, cut Maria from the whipping post.

The sheriff turned and addressed the councilmen as he dropped the cat. "Goody Jordan has a point. I'll not be a party to murder."

The deputies threw Maria on the back of an ox cart and took her to the town limits. A number of people followed along, and behind them, she could see the occasional reflection of Diablo from the glint of his silver tack and astride him the vague form of his rider. The driver tipped the cart, dumping Maria on the ground along with her pitiful bundle of belongings as the crowd jeered. The Sutton twins walked by and spat on her.

As she lay on the ground, Maria held clods of earth in her hands and clenched her fists. She felt the burning sensation of the welts and open lesions on her back and allowed herself to feel the full intensity of her pain. She felt wronged and wanted revenge. Then she cried, and as she did so, she heard the sound and smell of the presence of a horse standing near her. She finally turned her head. There stood Diablo and Bartholomew Ryder.

"You've had a bit of a time of it, lassie," he said as he dismounted.

"Yes, and you did nothing. The only person to do anything was Liza, and now she's in trouble."

"I wouldn't worry about your sister. What she said about murder is true, and all the good little Christians intent on beating you to a pulp are probably on their knees begging for the Lord's forgiveness. Most of them are probably soiling their britches at the thought they may not get into heaven and have a seat beside God looking down on the rest of us burning in hell."

Maria couldn't help but laugh at such an image. She could imagine Mr. Pratt waking up and praying with his pants full of excrement. She looked at Mr. Ryder and said, "You were there. Why didn't you help me?"

"Well, lassie, there were any number of places where I thought I could be useful, but I'm unable to act without a contract."

"But I have nothing, and I don't know what to ask for."

"That's something you need to decide on your own, but in the meantime, we need to take care of your immediate needs. Do you know what day it is?"

Maria hadn't been keeping track of the days since her father threw her out, and she strained to think. "Why, it's Halloween," she said.

"Bah, you Christians are all alike. Try again."

"It has to be Halloween, the time the dead and the devil roam the countryside." Then she looked at Mr. Ryder more closely and said, "Are you the devil?"

"I'm asked that from time to time, but let's work on how a contract would be in your best interest. But just to answer my question, it's not Halloween or any of that other Christian drivel." Then Mr. Ryder squatted down next to her and said, "It's Samhain. The time when the curtain between the living and the dead and the past and the future is the thinnest. Maybe I can show it to you. You have to be brave, but first, you must be thirsty." He lifted her head, and Maria drank wine poured into a silver cup he took from the saddlebag. Once she started to drink, she couldn't stop, and she drained the entire cup and another. Her last memory was of being wrapped in a cloak and being carried.

CHAPTER EIGHT

Maria didn't know if it was a dream because it seemed real. She could feel her mother's touch and smell her. Cuddling in bed, she felt warm and secure in her mother's arms. Then, she was standing on the deck of a ship, and she could see Sam commanding other men. He was a captain, and he had acquired considerable treasure. She could hear him speak to the other men of his love of a young woman in New England, Maria. Later, alone in the captain's cabin, she could feel his touch, and he kissed her. It felt real, like no other dream she had ever had.

When she woke up, she found herself in a bed. She looked around and saw that she lay in a shed-like structure made of boards and driftwood. The boards were weathered, and upon closer examination, she could see that they were planks from a ship's deck. Ship's knees were angled to support a collection of spars and reshaped masts securing the roof. Outside, she could hear the surf in the distance. She saw a table and two chairs, probably salvaged from a wreck. At first, she thought no one was about, but then Liza appeared. She didn't know if Liza was part of a dream, but she became real enough when she sat next to Maria and offered her a cup of water. Parched, she drank quickly.

"Where am I?" she asked.

"You're in a dune shack built by Ben. We come here sometimes to have some privacy, which we can't get in the cottage. He built it out of whatever he could find that washed up on the beach. The shack is deep in the dunes, so no one will bother you. You can use it until Sam fetches you or however long you want it."

"But Liza, how did I get here?"

"Ben and I brought you. We waited until the rest of the villagers left and wrapped you in a blanket. Then Ben carried you here, and I've been with you all night."

"But what about Mr. Ryder?"

"Who?"

"You know, Liza, the man with the big black horse. You can't have missed him. He gave me something to drink."

"Maria, we were with you all night from the time the trial started until now, and we didn't see a black horse or rider. But you were delirious when Ben picked you up. You babbled on and talked to Mama, and then you started talking to Sam. You seemed very happy, but enough of that, let me check your back. You must be in pain; I have some salve I can put on it."

"Liza, it doesn't hurt. It feels fine."

"You've always been a tough one. Just roll over and let me see."

Maria rolled over, and Liza put her hands on her back. She ran her fingers on Maria's spine and said, "This is strange. The cat caused angry welts across your back, and some of them were bleeding. I know because I saw and felt them last night, but now there is no sign of any injury."

"That's because Mr. Ryder, the man with the black horse, gave me something to drink, and it must have healed me. And then I saw Mom and Sam. They were real!"

"Maria, a lot has happened over the past few days, and without eating and the beating you took, no wonder you're seeing and hearing things. But now we need to get something into you to feed you and that babe. I'll stay with you for the next two days, but then I've got to get back. Don't worry. I'll be back every few days to bring you something and make sure you're safe."

After Liza left, Maria found her way to the beach, which proved arduous because her path was blocked by high dunes. She climbed one, but for each two steps she took, she slid back one step. Once at the top, she had a panoramic view of the beach and waves that rolled over hidden sand bars and crashed onto the beach. When she looked to the west, she saw a depression of several acres dominated by a marsh filled with high grass and cattails. Surrounding the marsh was a dense forest of white cedar and scrub pine, and in the center, she could see what she later discovered was a spring.

As the day went on, she found that

the marsh was in proximity to the shack, and a small path led to the spring. Maria got lost wandering among the grass and the cedar trees. She found if she blinked or turned quickly, one tree would look like another. Finally, she recognized a trail that led her back to the shack.

Maria liked living in the shack now that she was familiar with her way to the beach and the spring in the marsh. With winter closing in, she gathered driftwood from the beach for the small hearth where she could cook a simple meal. Her shack was cozy, and she was enjoying her pregnancy. The babe within her started to move, and she thought of her babe as company in her isolated surroundings.

A few days after she settled in, she heard the snorting of a horse, and she looked through a crack in the door. "Good day," said Mr. Ryder with a broad smile that seemed less than genuine to Maria.

"I've come to see how you're doing and to offer my services. Living by yourself, I fear that you'll need some protection."

Maria cut him short. "How is it that Sam didn't see you when you walked with me to Chatham, and Liza and Ben didn't see you the night I was cast out?"

"Strange. They should have seen me. Perhaps they weren't looking hard enough."

"I think they were looking very hard. And what was in that wine you gave me?"

"Isn't that wine interesting? It has a wonderful taste, but one has to be careful not to drink too much. It could result in disastrous consequences. I'm leaving a bottle for you in case you need it." Ryder pushed the bottle across the table and patted Maria on the shoulder, which felt less than reassuring to her.

"For what? And do I have to sign

in blood or something?" she said, leaning forward with both hands on the table.

"Oh no, Miss, this is strictly a gesture of goodwill, and the notion of signing in blood is made up by those troublesome Christians. This whole story about using an iron pen to sign in blood in a big book is all made up to discredit any dealings with forces on the other side of the curtain. I deal in verbal contracts, and if you wish further support from me, a simple handshake will do. As I said, my services can be attained on a promise of future goods and services. You can decide now or later, but in a few days, the rift in the Samhain curtain will be closing, and I'll be away for some time." He tipped his hat and smiled again.

Hours after Mr. Ryder departed, Maria heard a disturbance. Unsure who it might be, she crept around a large dune not far from her door. Three teenage girls stumbled around the sides of the shack. Two of them supported a girl between them who swayed, almost falling.

"Maria Hallett, we need your help. We heard in the village that you have healing powers, and Pearl is injured," said one girl as she continued to steady Pearl.

Maria looked at the girl who was being supported. She had a badly burned hand and face. "I don't know how to help. Where did you hear such a tale?"

"We met a man riding a black horse on the road near the village. He said you could help. Please, we were rendering fat to make tallow when the pot spilled, and Pearl was burned," said one of the girls.

Pearl then added, sobbing, "I'm ugly now, and the pain is bad, and I know now that John will never want to marry me."

Maria was unsure what to do, but

the girls had come from Chatham, and it would be difficult for Pearl to walk back along the sand, so she invited them in. Pearl sat on the bed and seemed ready to fall unconscious. Maria, acting on impulse, filled a glass half with water and half with the wine from the bottle Mr. Ryder had given her.

Soon after taking a few swallows, Pearl seemed to be energized. "The pain is going away," she said.

"It's the best I can do. I'm no healer," said Maria, surprised at how quickly the wine took effect.

The girls left, and Maria thought little of the incident. She knew the girls from the village and always thought them a bit silly. She figured the wine would support Pearl on the way home.

CHAPTER NINE

At twilight the same day, Maria smelled smoke coming from the beach. Dark clouds were heavy with rain pushed from the east by gale-force winds that snatched sand from the tops of the dunes, causing a stinging sensation if they touched exposed skin. Curious, she made her way through the dunes, and as she crested the top of the last one, she saw several men on the beach. She didn't know most of them, but she was surprised to see Pratt in charge.

"Make sure you make the fire look like the light to the entrance to the Chatham cut," she heard him say as the east wind blew the sound of his voice toward her.

Crouching low, Maria watched

them build the fire ever brighter, and with her back to the setting sun, she could see a sail lit by the dying light. She didn't know the differences between various ships, but large breaking seas were punishing a small two-masted bark. The ship turned toward the light. Too late, the skipper realized his ship was running upon a shoal. The ship turned once more, but the wind and surf were too strong. The squall intensified, and Maria lost sight of the ship for several minutes as the pelting rain obscured her vision. When she saw the ship again, it had struck fast upon a sandbar. With a cracking sound, her masts snapped like twigs and fell over the side. A breaking wave hit her so hard it sounded like an explosion, and it rolled on her side. More cracking sounds and desperate calls from the crew were audible over the sound of the gale as the ship broke up.

Pratt rubbed his hands. "Much booty tonight, boys. It's always a surprise to see what she's carrying. What a pity there'll be no survivors." Two sailors made their way through the surf. They were knee-deep in the swirling water when Pratt beckoned them to come toward him. "This way, fellows. We've a warm fire for you." As they approached Pratt, he hefted a cudgel and hit the first man square in the face, instantly dropping him. The second man made a run for his life up the beach but was caught by two of Pratt's confederates, the drunken Sutton twins, who clubbed him to death and rolled the body back into the surf. "Get what you can, boys. By morning, the whole township will be here picking over her bones. Take only what you think is most valuable, and take as much as you can carry. We'll be back with wagons in the morning."

Pratt turned toward the dunes, and Maria ducked her head too late. He had seen some movement. "Jack, Tom! There's somebody up there in the dunes. Find them, and then you know what to do."

Maria remembered how the twins cheered the loudest at her flogging and spit on her when she was dumped at the town line. She ran to the marsh near the dunes, a perfect hiding place since she now knew it well. Hiding among the reeds, she could occasionally hear the twins during lulls in the wind as they stumbled in the rain and dark in muck up to their knees. Drunk, they had no plan and fell several times. Tom thought he saw Maria in the shadows and lunged headfirst to tackle her. He was mistaken and rammed headlong into the stump of a long-dead tree. He lay there motionless, his face buried in the muck. Maria approached and could see he wasn't moving. As she came closer, she detected a slight stirring. It wasn't clear if Tom was regaining consciousness or if this was the movement of the water in the marsh. She couldn't take the chance of him reviving, so she stepped on the back of his head, pushing his face further into the muck, and waited several minutes until small bubbles appeared around his head.

In the meantime, Jack stumbled around, getting more frustrated over a lack of reply from his brother. Finally, he bellowed, "Since you're such an ass and probably in a stupor as usual, I'm leaving. You'll have to make your own way back to Chatham, and I'm keeping your share of the loot."

Carrying her child, Maria was exhausted, hungry, and shivering, and she wanted to get back to the shack. She approached the small dwelling and made a circular reconnaissance before entering. On the table was the dagger that Liza had used at the whipping post. It was the only defense she had, and she picked it up. Suddenly, her ears were ringing, and she was sitting on the ground, trying to make sense of what had happened as her vision and hearing slowly returned.

"Nice to meet you, Miss," she heard Jack say. "Thought you could outsmart old Jack. Once I saw this place, I knew whoever lived here would return. What a surprise to see a little bitch like you. I can't wait to take what you gave to that sailor lad so freely."

"If you touch me, Sam will carve you into little pieces when he gets back," she said, as she fumbled about on the floor for the dagger.

"Looking for this, Miss?" He waved the dagger in front of her face. Maria slid on her bottom to the farthest corner of the shack. "Oh, look at that. Who'd think that you'd be so considerate to provide a cup or two of wine before we get down to business." Jack didn't bother with the cup, but he pulled the cork out of the wine bottle with the few teeth he had left. He jammed the dagger into the table and took a long pull.

"Excellent stuff. I think I'll have another," and he took a swig, this time upending the bottle. "Excellent," he said again. "I wish I saved a drop for later." He wiped his sleeve across his mouth and took a step toward Maria. Then he clutched his throat. "Water!" he croaked, his eyes bulging as he stumbled about the shack, spilling a few of Maria's possessions on the floor, frantically searching for something to cool his throat.

"There's no water here," said Maria. "If you want some, you need to get it from the spring in the marsh."

Wheezing, Jack bolted from the shack. Maria reached under her bed for a jug and took several swallows of water she had drawn from the spring earlier.

CHAPTER TEN

Maria waited until sunrise, fearing that Jack would return. When he didn't, she left the shack and saw his tracks leading to the spring. Dagger in hand, she followed them. To her surprise, he wasn't near the spring, but for some reason, known only to him, had scrambled to the top of a dune. Maria could see that his skin was white and bloodless. She poked him with the dagger, and he didn't move. Maria had seen other dead people and knew he had joined them. She gave the corpse a swift kick, and it tumbled down the other side of the dune, creating a sand slide that covered the body.

Later, she observed the townspeople salvaging the wreck. There were several bodies lined up just above the waterline, including the two that Pratt had murdered. The people on the beach were too engrossed in salvaging what they could to pay much attention to Maria. She glanced away in disgust when she saw Pratt making a fuss over the wreck.

"This is a tragedy," he said. "Better navigation markers could probably have saved her. It's a shame; a ship destroyed, and at least ten good men lost their lives." Maria was about to speak up until she noticed that half of the people on the beach had been there the night before. She wisely held her tongue.

Due to the wreck's proximity and the recent visit from the girls, the location of her shack was now known. She took nothing from the wreck, but as she walked the water's edge, she locked eyes with Pratt. Her body went stiff, and for a moment, she couldn't move. His scowl and penetrating stare were the embodiment of evil, and he knew she had been the person on the dunes last night. She ran to the shack and held the dagger, hoping it would be of use against a grown man, but no one came to the shack until near sunset. To the east, there was still enough light from the setting sun so that she could make out Pratt approaching the cottage. His face was grim. In his left hand, he held the same dagger Sam had nipped the point off, and in his right, the cudgel that he used to kill the sailor. Maria was in a panic. Maybe she could offer him some of the wine she now regarded as magic, but the bottle had been drained by Jack Sutton.

"I'm coming for you, Miss," he shouted as he strode closer. "You'll be buried so deep in the dunes that no one will find you."

Then she heard the snorting of

a horse. Mr. Ryder and Diablo were silhouetted against the setting sun, and for a change, she was not the only one to see him. Pratt stopped, his expression changing from vengeance to fear. Maria heard a rasping sound as Mr. Ryder drew his saber. He urged Diablo forward at a trot with a pistol in his right hand and the saber in his left.

"Who are you?" shouted Pratt over his shoulder as he turned and ran.

Ryder said nothing, and at a canter, Diablo caught up to Pratt. Mr. Ryder's saber flashed and glinted in the rays of the setting sun as he swung it at Pratt, hitting him in the head with the flat of the blade and knocking him off his feet. He cocked his pistol and motioned for Pratt to get up. Mr. Ryder played with Pratt like a cat playing with a mouse and knocked Pratt down twice more until he chased him over the final dune before the beach. He returned to the cottage and dismounted.

"That was thirsty work," he said as he poured a full cup of wine from the empty bottle, then took a long swallow and dabbed his lips with a handkerchief. "That was a near thing, Miss, but I can't keep intervening without a contract. Mr. Pratt is bound to get drunk sometime and tell all about this encounter, and then there is that silly girl, Pearl. You know her face is perfectly healed. Some in town are coming to believe you're a witch. Oh, and then there are the Sutton twins moldering away in the marsh. That needs explaining as well, and the only conclusion the good Christians in town will come to is that it's the work of a witch, including the wreck of that bark."

For a brief time, Maria sat speechless. She didn't believe that such things could happen. "You know all of what you do is witchcraft, but I'm no witch. You make these things happen," she finally blurted out.

"Now, there is where you're incorrect, Miss. I didn't create any of those situations. I just provided solutions. You're free not to take my offer, but I would say two things: You can run away, but I fear a young lady in your condition wouldn't get far and would either perish or be taken advantage of by some unscrupulous scoundrel. The other consideration is that the villagers' fear of witchcraft will be stoked by Mr. Pratt. I don't think they'd burn you at the stake. Burning tends to be a European solution to the witchcraft problem, but as we know from what happened in Salem a few years back, hanging and pressing are still viable options."

"I have nothing," she said, covering her face to hide her tears.

"Like I said, services or goods to be paid at a later date," he said, extending his hand. "The Samhain curtain is closing, and by the winter solstice, I must away."

Maria extended her hand, and as she withdrew it, a slight cut appeared on her index finger. "Now drink this, and the contract is sealed," Mr. Ryder poured two cups from the bottle, and they drank.

CHAPTER ELEVEN

Maria fell into a deep sleep, and she saw wonderful visions of Sam's return and watched her child grow into a fine young man. However, as she drank more of the wine over the following weeks, Maria had vague nightmares that would break through her pleasant dreams. She glimpsed a young boy with a face like her beloved's being led to the gallows. She had no memory of the exact content of these dreams, but they left her with the feeling that both Sam and her babe were facing dreadful peril.

Over the next months, she had few encounters with the townsfolk or with Mr. Pratt, who kept his pirating well away from the coast near her cottage. She told all to Liza, who was overwhelmed and not sure how she could help. "Whatever you did for Pearl has gotten around the village. Some see you as a healing witch. It's likely you'll have other visitors."

What Liza said was true, and Maria sent most people seeking aid away, but if she thought she could help, she would offer the person a taste of her wine. She had no idea how it worked and never viewed herself as a witch. When her time came, she gave birth to a healthy boy with only Liza's help, and she named him Joseph. Liza stayed with her and Joseph for a week. The day after she left, a nor'easter blew in and rattled her little shack. She rocked Joseph to comfort him. Above the sound of the wind, she heard the sound of a horse approaching. She peeked through a crack in the boards and watched Mr. Ryder dismount and knock on the door.

"Well, Miss, it seems things are

going smoothly, and it's time to discuss payment," he said.

"I still have nothing except for a few coins that people gave me for being cured by your wine. You're welcome to them."

"Ah yes, I'm afraid that the price is higher than that, and you do have something of value," he said, looking at Joseph.

Her face drained of color, and she felt dizzy. "No! You can't have him. I love him, and you can't take an infant from his mother," she said, hugging Joseph close.

"Quite so. If you remember, 'goods or services to be paid at a later date.' He's still suckling, but there'll be a time when he'll no longer require your breast, and I'll be back, so be ready."

"How can you be so cruel? Is there no other payment that can be made?"

"There are always alternative

arrangements that can be made, but in your case, I don't see any options. So, in a year's time, Miss."

CHAPTER TWELVE

While I was entering the library, I received the report on the blood from my friend at the university lab and listened on my mobile. "Hey Joe, I got some interesting news and some creepy news," he said.

"So, are you going to hold me in suspense? Just spit it out," I said.

"Well, first of all, your suspicions were correct. It isn't ink on those pages. It's human blood."

"Seems creepy."

"No, that's the interesting part. The creepy part is still to come. We have some new techs in the lab, and instead of turning them loose right away on projects funded by the university, we decided to use your samples to test out a new hire."

"You're talking in circles. What's

the point?"

"We used your samples as part of the training regimen for DNA analysis. Turns out, our new staff is crackerjack, and whoever owned the other sample is closely related to you. The sample is female, and you're a direct descendant."

I hung up, turned, and headed to the pub. I needed another three drinks to clear my mind after that bit of news. I was about to order when I heard the rumble of that Chevy SS, and Bart came through the door, taking a seat next to me at the end of the bar.

"You drink the Powers if I remember," he said as he waved to Riley. "Make it two, both with ice on the side."

"So, did you manage to break through the curtain to visit us from the other side," I said with more than a little sarcasm.

"Nope, it's too far past Samhain, so

I'm stuck on this side until it rolls around again," he laughed. "You look a little distressed."

I drained my glass of Powers and said, "I've just found out that I'm a DNA match to a long-dead author that I don't know the name of."

"That sounds like something to celebrate. Who's the author?" Bart smiled, not acknowledging that he was aware of the book.

"I can't even tell you the title. There isn't one. It's just a convoluted story about the wreck of the *Whydah*."

"Aha, I know it well. There's quite a love story between 'Black' Sam Bellamy and what's her name?"

"Maria Hallett."

"Right, you know there's a mystery connected to the wreck. Some say that Bellamy drowned, but others say that he and Maria disappeared along with their son and treasure," Bart said as he watched the whiskey curtain in the tumbler before he took a sip. "But there's also a curse since it's alleged there was cargo aboard of, let's say, of religious interest that has special power. And worse, apparently, Maria reneged on a deal, and a curse has followed her line since then and will continue until the debt is paid."

"How would you know?"

"Well, I'm a historian and, like I said, in the collection business to make ends meet. Bartender, another round. I've learned that paying debts is an important virtue, and sometimes debts can extend over generations with the interest building if it isn't paid. My reading of various contracts that are held by interests on the other side are never terminated with the person taking out the loan passing away because time on the other side is ethereal and is both stretched and compressed. As a result, some poor slob centuries later can be hit with quite a bill."

"Oh, come on, this whole thing you're suggesting is just bull," I said.

"Well, take it as you may, but if you find you're stuck with the debt, it's best to pay up before something awful happens."

I sat on the bar stool dumbfounded, trying to determine how what Bart said to me would figure into my life. To help me think more clearly, I had another three whiskeys after he left. The next morning, I was under the weather again.

The wife was not pleased. "Most of the time when you go to the pub, you have a few and come home in a good mood. But this is the second time Riley has had to put you into a cab. He says that the last two times you've been in, you sat at the end of the bar, mumbling to yourself. He has no recollection of seeing 'The Man in Black' or a black hot rod. I've made an appointment for you to see Sue Miller. She's a therapist, and they say she's very good."

I was now on a mission. First off, I lied to Dr. Miller and told her anything she wanted to hear. "Yes, Doctor, it must be the booze, and I promise to cut back. It's nice of you to suggest AA, but I keep forgetting to go. I promise I'll go next week."

What was more important was spending more time in the library consulting the book and going to the town hall to get acquainted with my ancestors. Since my family has lived on the Cape since colonial times, it was possible to track down most of my lineage, although it got muddled the further back I went. As I tracked my maternal line, the surnames kept changing as these pesky women kept getting married. Some of them got married more than once as their husbands passed away, complicating the search.

However, there was a more disturbing trend, and that was that any boy with the given name Joseph wound up living a turbulent life, sometimes being diagnosed with mental illness, experiencing delusions of persecution, or hearing voices that told them what to do. Deaths through suicide and violent accidents were common in their histories.

CHAPTER THIRTEEN

For the next year, Maria's life didn't change much. She loved watching Joseph grow and spent hours playing with him. Liza made regular visits. At bedtime, Maria would occasionally take a sip of wine, which led to dreams of Sam. In her dreams, he was now a successful pirate, and her dreams about him were confirmed by Liza's visits.

"He's now known as 'Black' Sam Bellamy, the Robin Hood of pirates," Liza told her. "You know they'll hang him all the same when they catch him. Are you sure you want to go away with him?"

"I know he loves me because I see him in my dreams, and what you tell me confirms my dreams."

It was getting near Joseph's first

birthday, and she feared that Ryder would take Joseph from her. She told Liza of her predicament, and Liza said, "Sister, what you tell me is hard to believe, but then they say you cured that silly girl, Pearl, and have helped many others. I know you, and before you met Sam, you had no special powers other than avoiding chores."

"I still don't. Any power is in that wine bottle. I just give a glass to people I think need it, and it seems to work. But I'm afraid that Joseph will be taken from me. I know Mr. Ryder will be back. I don't know what to do."

"I have an idea. I'll take Joseph. He knows me and Ben, and I know Ben would never let harm come to Joseph."

CHAPTER FOURTEEN

Joseph turned fifteen months old and started to give up nursing. It was at this time that Maria reluctantly gave Joseph to Liza.

Liza spoke to Joseph as she cuddled him. "Don't worry, my baby. It'll only be a short time, and you'll be back with Mama." Then she reassured Maria. "Ben has relatives off the Cape. Your Mr. Ryder will never find him."

Liza took Joseph while he slept, and within two days, Mr. Ryder appeared. "It's time, Miss. I'll allow you some time to say goodbye to your babe," he said in a cold, demanding manner he had not used before.

"He's not here, Mr. Ryder, and even if he were, I would never give my child away," she said as she locked eyes with Ryder.

Mr. Ryder's face transformed into a distorted scowl. "You have no idea what forces you're unleashing. You're violating the contract, and the interest will continue to build. Payment will only be more painful for you. I can offer Joseph a spectacular life. He'll be well-educated and be able to support you in a style you can't begin to imagine. You're making a big mistake."

Maria stiffened. "You're a liar, Mr. Ryder. With the help of your wine, I've had dreams that pulled back that curtain, and they show that Joseph being turned to evil, and I can't allow that. There is nothing you can do to me to give my flesh and blood to you."

"You'll be sorry, and your seed will be punished for generations to come if you don't give Joseph to me."

"Get out and never come back.
Your contract means nothing to me.
You manipulated me, and your price is
unfair." Maria snatched the dagger from
the table, and to make her point, she
raised it above her head and drove it into
the table, missing Ryder's fingers by a
hair.

Ryder looked her in the eyes, calmly
raising an eyebrow, and said, "They all
say that. You'll pay one way or another.
You'll see."

Maria fell on her knees, hugging
herself after Ryder left. She reached for
the bottle of wine for some fortification,
but when she opened the bottle, the liquid
smelled foul, and she fell unconscious
from the stench. In her dream, she saw
the *Whydah,* and she was wrecked like the
little bark, and in the same location. When
she woke up, there was more bad news.
Liza banged on her door. "The Sutton

twins were found in the marsh, and Mr. Pratt is placing the responsibility of their deaths on you. He says it's witchcraft. He wants the town fathers to have a trial and have you hanged. They denied his claim for lack of evidence, but it seems that even that silly girl Pearl is accusing you, since her face is showing signs of scarring that is getting worse. My guess is that in a week, they'll arrest you."

"Then I'll put some things together and slip away tonight. Perhaps Ben's people will take me in."

"You can't leave too soon, but it may be wise to put travel off for a day because bad weather is coming in. You should hide in the dunes or marsh until tomorrow night."

As Maria left the shack for the marsh, the wind once again blew at gale force, ripping sand from the tops of the dunes and mixing it with raindrops that stung her face. She thought about her dream of the wreck of the *Whydah* and realized that the circumstances were similar. She decided to go to the beach. What she saw was a confirmation of her nightmares. She looked over the crest of the last dune and partly covered her eyes from the east wind and rain. Mr. Pratt was directing the feeding of a fire beacon, and next to him, astride Diablo, sat Bartholomew Ryder.

CHAPTER FIFTEEN

Black Sam Bellamy stood with legs spread to balance himself on the pitching quarterdeck of the *Whydah,* snapping out orders. For a change, the crew responded without complaining or quarreling about alternative ways to handle the ship. This was not the normal way the day-to-day running of a pirate ship was handled. Under most conditions related to sailing the ship or deciding on a destination, the decision was put to a vote. It was only during combat conditions that the elected captain had unquestioned command of the ship. But the *Whydah* and her crew were not experiencing normal conditions, so they obeyed Sam's orders without questioning his authority.

The last three days had been hell,

although the first day didn't start that way. Sailing up the coast of the British colonies had been a pleasure, with good sailing weather pushing them north and the added opportunity, Sam thought, to take prizes. Their luck changed when the *Whydah* encountered the *Mary Anne* off the coast of Connecticut, a hundred-ton galley from Glasgow bound for New York, loaded with Madeira wine and other spirits. They also captured the *Fisher*, a coastal sloop with a cargo of beer. Both ships also carried rum and whiskey. They sailed in company, but as the weather changed, the *Mary Anne* and the *Fisher* were lost in the fog.

Before they were separated by the fog, the *Whydah*'s crew transferred as much of the wine and related spirits at sea by the ship's boats. The arrival of the spirits improved the mood of the crew, but didn't improve their judgment. Even the newest member of the crew, John King, a ten-year-old boy, managed to get stupefyingly drunk and passed out like most of the crew.

Sam managed to stay reasonably coherent, and as he looked to the south, he could see dark clouds building into thunderheads with black underbellies. Now in his mid-twenties, he had gone to sea when he too was ten years old, and he knew that the clouds were a bad omen. He staggered to his feet and took two steps, falling flat on his back. His usual surefooted ability to navigate a pitching deck had deserted him as the *Whydah* started to rock unpredictably in an increasingly choppy sea. He rolled across the deck until he came to rest against a rope coiled between two cannons. Within the coil, curled in a fetal position, lay John King. Sam rolled to his hands and knees and looked at John. At first, he thought the lad might be dead due to his pale complexion. He grabbed the boy by the shoulder and shook him. John stirred slightly, moaned, vomited, and curled himself into a tighter ball.

Damn, thought Sam, the little rascal is useless. He's too small to help handle the sheets and halyards. But he had to give John credit because the brat was fearless when climbing the rigging like a monkey, and his young eyes made him an excellent lookout... if you could get him to pay attention for more than a few minutes without having to boot him in the behind.

CHAPTER SIXTEEN

Sam sat and collected his thoughts before he had to roust some of the crew who might be sober enough to function. He reflected on how John King had joined the ship.

Before the *Whydah* became a pirate ship, she had been a slaver. She had delivered her cargo of slaves and was heading to Europe loaded with cash and wealthy passengers when she was cornered by Sam and his gang, who quickly realized her speed and size, as well as heavy armament, made her an ideal instrument to plunder shipping coming or leaving the Americas. With her hull full of booty, the crew voted to sail north to Nova Scotia, where it was rumored that pirates were welcomed and could purchase a pardon.

On the way north, the *Whydah* captured a merchantman carrying the kind of ship's stores the crew would need for the trip north, as well as more wealthy passengers. The pirates plundered the cargo and relieved the passengers of their valuables. Needing a ship's carpenter, they pressed the merchantman's carpenter into service against his will by showing him the skull and pistol. Because it was also the policy of the pirate crew to recruit crew members from the captured vessel, Sam stood before the crew and passengers of the captured ship with a pair of pistols in his belt, his hand resting on the hilt of the cutlass that hung on his hip.

"Who would like to join the company of our fine ship? Every man jack of *Whydah*'s crew has an equal share of the booty. As a result, we are all rich, and when we go ashore, we can live the life of a gentleman for the rest of our lives. All you have to do is put your mark saying you agree to abide by the ship's articles."

"Aye, and get our necks stretched by the King's men when they catch up with us," said a voice from the crowd.

"Ha, the life of a gentleman," said another. "But for how long?"

Sam spun about and confronted the sailors, who commented as he adjusted the brace of pistols in his belt. "Aye, like I said, you'll live the life of a gentleman, but I never said for how long your life might be."

Lubricated by the spirits liberated from the captain's cabin, the pirate crew and some of the prisoners broke out in laughter.

"So, who's for the pirate's life?" Sam repeated, brandishing his cutlass.

All the potential recruits refused

to make eye contact and stared at their feet or up into the rigging, except one. A scrawny ten-year-old boy, one of the passengers, stepped forward.

"I'll sign the articles," he said with a steady gaze, suggesting that he meant what he said.

"And who might I be addressing?" said Sam, staring at the lad.

"I'm John King," the boy said, thrusting out his chest.

"No! Please, no! Please, captain, don't take my boy," said a woman as she stepped between John and Sam.

Before anyone could lay a hand on the boy, he ran in the opposite direction, shot up the rigging like a spider running across its web, and sat on the lower yard of the mainmast.

Kneeling as if she were in prayer, his mother looked up. "Please come down," she begged.

"No, Mum. I want to be a pirate. And when I come back as a gentleman, I'll buy you a house with servants on the richest street in London."

As she groveled on the deck, Sam felt compassion for her. He scanned his crew until he locked eyes with Silas Wilson, the best topman of the entire crew.

"Up you go, and bring the lad back to his mum," said Sam, motioning with his head for Silas to start climbing the rigging.

Silas was a fit young man with broad shoulders and callused hands from spending so much time aloft. He shot up the rigging as fast as the boy had, but by the time he reached the lower yard, the lad had secured a line that connected with the mizzen mast and had gone hand over hand from the main mast to the mizzen top. Silas was equal to the task, but every time he had John cornered, the lad would make an insane leap to a different stay or halyard. When Silas got above him, John would descend to a lower part of the rigging, and when Silas descended, the lad would scamper past him to a higher perch.

The crews from both vessels and the passengers started to cheer, and wagers were made about if and when the lad would be captured. Finally, Silas had John cornered on the end of the top yard of the main mast.

"Come on, lad. It was a merry chase, but it's time to go down to your mum." Silas extended his hand.

No one had been paying attention to the behavior of the *Whydah* or the merchantman as they drifted near each other in a mild five-knot breeze. The two vessels drifted together, gently touching and brushing against each other's rigging. John didn't hesitate, and like a flying squirrel, he leaped from the rigging to the *Whydah*, catching one of the shrouds supporting the main mast, and clambered up to the main top yard.

On the deck of the merchantman, Sam could hear a murmur amongst his crew. The quartermaster, Mr. Stevens, pushed his way past the other crew and said to Sam, "We had a vote and decided that if the lad wants to sign the articles, we should let him."

Sam didn't agree with the vote, and he felt bad about leaving John's mum sobbing on the deck of the merchantman as *Whydah* set her sails and headed north. But there was nothing he could do. *Whydah* functioned as a democracy, and he, like his crew, had to abide by the ship's articles.

Sam had been surprised at how well John fit in with the crew. Mr.

Stevens taught him how to be a powder monkey and bring powder and ball from the magazine when the cannons were fired. John also learned to load and shoot a pistol, as well as the fine art of sliding a dagger between an enemy's ribs. But the biggest surprise was that he could read and do sums, so Sam took it upon himself to teach John navigation.

CHAPTER SEVENTEEN

Sam shook his head to bring himself back to the present. A cold rain interrupted his thoughts as the weather front gathered speed, rapidly overtaking the *Whydah*. The black clouds were accompanied by an increasing number of lightning strikes that caused them to glow like Japanese lanterns. Sam watched a gust of wind race toward the ship, tearing the tops off the waves. It struck her on the starboard beam like a giant cannon, causing the *Whydah* to be knocked down. He, along with anything not tied down, slid across the deck, landing against the port side where water gushed through the scuppers. A loud cracking sound drew his attention, and as he looked up, he could see the top half of the main mast come crashing down, part of which landed on the deck while the remainder was lost overboard. He heard a scream that was cut short, and he never found out who it was.

The shattered mast turned out to be a blessing because it lowered the pressure of the wind that was forcing *Whydah* on her beam end. Slowly, she started to right herself, but she was still in peril of capsizing and sinking if she didn't get her bow into the wind. The wind and cold rain had a sobering effect on the crew, and they needed no encouragement to get to their assigned posts. Some scrambled up the rigging to furl sails while others manned the sheets and halyards to lower as much rigging as possible. Two men manned the helm until they were knocked down, and two others took their place. Slowly, *Whydah* answered her helm, and she was able to ride steady, taking the wind and waves on her bow.

Sam knew they were a crack crew and as good or better than any warship's crew. This was because nearly every member of the crew was a volunteer selected by the crew, who voted on who would be allowed to sign the articles. If someone wanted to join the crew and they were sickly or a known slacker, they weren't allowed to sign. Besides, each member of the crew had an equal share of the booty, unlike on a naval ship, where the captain received the lion's share and the crew got a pittance or nothing at all. However, none of that mattered now because they knew their lives were at stake and they needed to work together to survive.

CHAPTER EIGHTEEN

For three days, they battled the storm. Sam had managed to con the ship, so she was running stern to the wind. *Whydah* also leaked badly due to the damage she had sustained, with her seams opening because of the stress of running downwind in heavy seas. Manning the pumps was backbreaking work, and all aboard knew pumping the bilge was the key to their survival. No one slept. Men manned the pumps or wrestled with the helm to keep *Whydah*'s stern to the breaking seas until they dropped from the exhaustion that counted as sleep.

Sam sat tied to a chair, wrapped in an oilskin cloak next to the helm so he could keep an eye on the ship's progress. Startled, he let out a snort when someone tugged his arm. He'd fallen asleep without realizing it. John King stood in front of him with a loaf of soggy bread, some cheese, and a tankard of hot rum. "Cook said you haven't eaten in over a day, and you should eat this."

Sam had not thought about food while trying to save the ship, but reminded by John, he felt ravenous. He bit off a large chunk of cheese and then took two mouthfuls of bread. He didn't care that the bread was soggy and the cheese moldy. Next, he drained the tankard of rum, chugging it all at once.

Looking at John, he thought the lad looked like a half-drowned rat. Someone in the crew had helped John braid his shoulder-length hair in a pigtail and tar it in sailor fashion. This caused rain and spray to collect and run onto the pigtail and down his back. His tricorn hat was comical because every time he tilted his head, water would run out one of the corners like tea from a kettle's spout. Sam shifted in his chair, allowing water to run off his oilskin cloak.

"So, lad, what have you been up to? We haven't had time for your lessons."

John pulled his soaking wool cloak around him. "Cook grabbed me and said I had the balance of an acrobat, and that made me the perfect person to bring victuals to the crew at their stations without spilling much. But what I want to know is, do you know our present position?"

Sam untied the lashings holding him to the chair and stood and looked into the binnacle holding the compass that gyrated with the ship's motion. "In these seas, it's hard to get an accurate fix. However, I can tell you that as the storm passes us, we've had to make major course changes to keep our stern to the wind. The wind is now blowing out of the east, meaning we are sailing due west and may wind up where we started three days ago. With the clouds and rain, it is impossible to get a noon fix from the sun or a nighttime fix from the stars."

John fingered the edge of his cloak. "Do you think we'll sink? If so, I hope we can launch one of the ship's boats because I can't swim, and the water is cold."

Sam put on a phony smile to help John feel more confident. "I wouldn't worry, John. The *Whydah* is a strong ship, and even with the beating she has taken, the pumps are keeping up with the water in the bilge."

He saw that John was starting to shiver, and his lips were blue. "As your captain, I'm ordering you back to the galley. Tell the cook I said you need to warm up, and you are not to leave the galley until you dry out and sleep."

John took a breath and started to protest, but Sam cut him off to distract the lad. "I learned to swim when I was about your age, and when we return to warmer waters, I'll teach you. Now git!" He saw John smile as he scampered off to the galley.

CHAPTER NINETEEN

Sam didn't like the notion of running west before the wind because visibility was less than a mile in fog, rain, and high wind. He went to his cabin, one of the dryer parts of the ship, and consulted charts of the New England waters taken from ships they had captured. He placed his finger on a location northeast of Cape Cod. "I think we are about here, Mr. Stevens."

Mr. Stevens was a big-boned man who spoke with an accent suggesting he could come from anywhere in the English-speaking world. As far as the crew knew, he didn't have a first name, so everybody referred to him as Mister. Besides Sam, he was the only one who knew how to navigate using a sextant. Mr.

Stevens cleared his throat. "I'm inclined to agree with you. If your position is correct, we could pass north of Race Point, the northern tip of the Cape, and if we turned south, we'd be in the lee of the Cape and out of this dreadful weather. But I worry that this chart is old, and the way the sand shifts around the Cape, it is probably inaccurate."

A crew member banged on the cabin door but didn't wait for a reply, stumbling through the entrance dripping wet. He blurted out, "The lad said he has sighted a coastline and says it looks like there is a beacon along the shore."

Mr. Stevens bolted from the cabin, grabbed a telescope from the chart table, and climbed halfway up the shrouds, where he found John, who had tied himself to some of the stays so he could keep his hands free. He shouted in John's ear to be heard over the wind and pounding waves. "What do you see, lad?"

John shouted back in Mr. Stevens' ear, "Two points off the starboard bow. I think there is a light."

Mr. Stevens took the telescope he had slung around his neck and braced it against one of the backstays. It was hard to determine if he was looking at a fog bank or land because both appeared gray at twilight. Then he caught a glimmer of a fire beacon. The lad had exceptional vision. "Good eyes," he shouted as he reached for a backstay and slid to the deck where Sam was waiting.

"It's a beacon for sure," he said.

Under the lee of the space between the main deck and the quarterdeck, Sam spoke with Mr. Stevens. He shook his head. "It looks like we miscalculated our position and are running smack into Cape Cod. Our only hope is that the beacon is the marker for the cut into Chatham Harbor."

Mr. Stevens leaned forward to be heard. "If we make it into the harbor, there will be hell to pay. We'll hang for sure."

Sam laughed and gave Stevens a playful nudge. "Let's think this through. We have a crew of over one hundred men who know how to fight, and *Whydah* has over thirty cannons. The last time I visited Chatham, they had a motley militia whose men were more interested in drinking at the tavern than drilling and learning how to fight, and they don't have any cannons. We could plunder the town in an hour if we desired. Chatham is also the home of my beloved." Sam rubbed his hands in anticipation of seeing Maria again. He had never told the crew, but his reason for sailing north was to find her and take her away with him.

CHAPTER TWENTY

Now Sam turned and rushed to the quarterdeck. After surveying the coast with this telescope, he commanded the helmsman, "Two points to the starboard. Steer for that light. Let's hope it's the Chatham beacon."

As he glanced into the rigging, he saw John rapidly slide down a backstay. When John reached the deck, he ran to the quarterdeck. "Shoals!" John shouted. "Nothing but shoals all the way to the beach!"

"Hard alee! Turn to the port," Sam shouted to the sailors manning the helm. The desperation in his voice indicated he didn't have to repeat the order.

Whydah's response was sluggish, and due to her missing topsails and sprung mainmast, she was deprived of the power to work to the windward. She was inexorably being drawn onto the shoal, but he knew they had one more chance.

"Deploy the anchor!" he shouted as he ran to the forecastle where the anchor was stowed and encountered two bewildered men, both holding sledgehammers. Sam didn't hesitate. He snatched a hammer from one of the men and swung it at the chock securing the anchor chain. It didn't budge, so he shouted to the man holding the other hammer, "For God's sake, hit the chock!"

The man snapped out of his trancelike state and alternated striking the chock with Sam. With the fourth blow, the chock came loose and shot across the deck, hitting a bystander in the shin and knocking him down. There was no time to attend to the injured man as they let out half of the anchor line before belaying it as it took hold. *Whydah* slowly responded, pointing her bow into the breaking waves, one of which broke over the forecastle and raced across the main deck, dislodging everything from belaying pins to broken spars and converting them into missiles that knocked men over until the water exited through the scuppers.

Sam took a deep breath, relieved that the ship was secure. Then he heard a call from one of the men in the rigging. "We're dragging, Captain!"

A glance confirmed that although *Whydah* was riding bow to the wind and sea, the coast and the beacon were getting bigger.

"Rig the second anchor!" shouted Sam. It took time to complete this task on a wildly pitching deck. He saw John standing on the perimeter of the men who were rigging the anchor. He took the lad by the arm and shouted in his ear, "John, go to my cabin, and in the bottom of my sea chest, you'll find a canvas bag with my share of the booty. I want you to take it and tie it to one of the oars in the ship's boat and stay there.

"Are we going to sink?" said John, his eyes tearing.

"I don't think so, but if disaster strikes, stay in the boat and cut the lashings so she'll float free. We should be safe," he lied.

Sam gave the order to deploy the second anchor and watched the line run out through the hawser. The line quickly became stiff and hard as an iron rod as the anchor set. The line groaned like it was in pain. The Samson post securing the bitter end of the anchor line tore from its fastenings. It raced across the deck, knocking one man overboard and smashing through the hawser pipe, leaving a large gap that allowed the breaking waves to flood onto the deck. At the same time, *Whydah* was lifted by a wave. It carried her onto a sandbar, where the stern smashed onto the ocean bottom, converting the mizzen mast into a pile driver that drove through the bottom of the stern and fractured the keel. Sam knew she was breaking up, and there was no way to save her. The sound of the falling rigging and smashing of the hull sounded to Sam like the *Whydah* was screaming in pain.

He ran to the ship's boat, which provided the only hope of survival. Looking in the boat, he saw the canvas bag secured to an oar, but John was nowhere in sight. Mr. Stevens, who was preparing the boat to be launched, looked up and said, "The lad said he had to go below and would be right back."

Sam shook his head in frustration. "I'm going to get the lad. Try not to leave without us." He knew it was a hopeless request because Stevens would launch the boat if he thought the conditions were right, regardless of whether Sam and John were with him.

Sam forced his way down the companionway past men struggling to escape the chaos below, clutching their booty and whatever possessions they thought might help save their lives. *Whydah* started to list to the point that she might capsize at any moment, and Sam had to descend the companionway with one foot on the ladder and the other on the bulkhead. Each time the ship was lifted by a wave, she was slammed on the hard sand bottom, creaking and groaning, her shattered planking allowing more seawater into her bilge.

The deck was miraculously lit

by a lantern with one candle swinging from an overhead beam, and Sam saw John knee-deep in bilgewater looking for something. John held up a box with the sextant in it that Sam had given him and smiled at Sam. On the upside of the listing ship, a cannon weighing over a ton was double-lashed to the ship's frame. It looked like the lashing would hold, but Sam heard what sounded like a scream as the retaining eye bolts were torn out of the timbers. In an instant, the cannon broke free and roared across the deck, sliding on its side and smashing anything in its path. The huge barrel struck John in the chest and continued to smash through the outer planks into the open sea as if John had never been in its way.

Sam knew that there was nothing he could do for John, who was likely killed instantly. He raced for the companionway as the incoming sea filled the lower deck, and like a giant hand, the water pushed him up the companionway like a cork out of a bottle. He slid across the deck on his hands and knees, colliding with rigging blocks, spars, and bodies. Some men were dead, and others were so injured that there was no hope for them: even a minor injury like a broken wrist could be a death sentence. Finding his way to the ship's boat, he could see that it was still lashed to the deck despite the ship's list. He feared that at any moment, one of the cannons on the high side of the deck would repeat what he had seen below.

His only chance was to cut the lashings to free her and float to safety. His optimism soon turned to disappointment as he grasped the boat's gunwale and looked inside. Mr. Stevens lay in the bilge, covered with broken spars and assorted cordage and rigging blocks. One hefty spar pierced his chest, making him look like a bug on display in a collector's case. Unfortunately, the spar also continued through her planking, rendering the boat useless.

As *Whydah* broke up, the sound of her cracking timbers and cries from the crew motivated Sam. He could see that she was ready to capsize since her lower spars were in the water, indicating she was lying on her side. Sam collected the oar that John had tied his bag to and then saw a toolbox floating in the boat's bilge. He dumped out the tools and closed the lid, locking it down by closing the hasp, forming an airtight box.

As he tried to abandon the ship, it appeared that she had other plans. He was buffeted with any debris that floated by, and cordage seemed like tentacles trying to pull him under. However, as he grasped the box and oar, a wave lifted him up into the breaking surf. Clearing the wreck, he could see the beacon. Despite the cold water, he knew that he had to avoid coming ashore near the beacon because whoever set the beacon was up to no good, and they would probably kill him. He decided to work his way north of the beacon, where the waves and tide seemed to be taking him. The surf battered him, sometimes pressing him against the bottom until he thought his lungs would burst. At other times, it would lift him to the top of a crest and slam him into the sand, causing him to let go of the box that had kept him afloat. Finally, he found that the surf was shallow enough that he could stand briefly before he was knocked down by a following wave. He still clung to the oar that enabled him to use it as a crutch as he staggered to the edge of the surf.

Resting briefly, Sam knew he had

to move off of the beach before whoever lit the false beacon discovered him. He hoped to hide in the dunes, and with luck, he might be able to contact Maria. He pulled a dagger from his belt, cut the bag from the oar, and limped toward the edge of the dunes.

CHAPTER TWENTY-ONE

Out beyond the breakers, Maria saw a ship much bigger than the small bark that had wrecked two years earlier, but the results were the same. She saw the ship strike the bar with a force that snapped her masts. The ship was now helpless as the sea and wind continued to wash her onto the shoals. She violently capsized, and the sound of heavy objects like cannons and ballast smashing through the decks and hull could be heard on the shore. The crowd of men on the beach cheered, and some men waded into the ferocious surf to grab some booty before it was buried in the sand or washed back out to sea. Maria saw a handful of survivors struggling ashore. They were allowed to reach the shore, and then she saw knives and cudgels rise and fall on them.

"Don't kill them all," called Pratt. "First, find out what ship she is, and then kill 'em."

A call came from down the beach, "This man says the ship is the *Whydah*, Sam Bellamy captain, and he was forced into piracy because they needed a carpenter."

"Aye, in that case, spare him and one or two others. We can hang 'em as pirates to show we're doing our civic duty. Get at it, boys. She must be loaded with treasure; she'll make us all rich."

Maria pushed her face into the sand. Her world and all her hopes were undone, and she was sure that Bartholomew Ryder was responsible. She felt helpless against such odds and decided that her only mission in life was to save Joseph from the clutches of Mr.

Ryder. She turned to go, and in doing so, she looked further up the beach toward Truro and Provincetown and away from the debris field. The salvors directed by Pratt were too busy getting what treasure they could to notice a lone figure emerging from the surf a quarter mile away. Maria, from her position on the dune, had a better view even though her sightline was occasionally obscured by sheets of rain and spray being torn from the tops of the waves.

She worked her way down the beach, and as she did, she could see the man had a rope tied around his waist and was pulling something from the surf. It looked like a broken oar with scraps of sailcloth still clinging to it. She was surprised that the man had strength enough to stand. Then, he drew a dagger and cut a heavy bag loose from the oar, and hauled it with him across the beach to the edge of the dunes, where he was hidden from the men on the beach. Maria made her way behind the dunes to a place where there was a passage to the beach. Peeking around the dune, she watched the man try to climb the dune.

She called to the man through the sound of the surf and wind. "It's much easier to take this passage than to try to climb over the dune and be exposed to the pirates down the beach. They already killed several of your shipmates."

"Thank you, Miss," he said in a hoarse voice. "We were deceived and thought that the light marked the Chatham cut. Do you have any water? I've swallowed so much seawater, I need some fresh."

As the man cleared his voice, Maria thought she recognized it.

"Sam," she said.

"Some say that's my name. And

yours?"

Excitement rose within her. Her faith wasn't misplaced. Black Sam Bellamy had come back for her. "Maria, Maria Hallett," she said.

Sam took her hand and pulled her toward him until she fell upon him. "I came for you with the intention of giving up pirating and offering you the life of a gentlelady. This isn't the way I intended to return." He kissed her, and they both lay shivering until Maria lifted her head and said, "We have to get off the beach and hide, or they'll kill you. We can hide in the marsh where there's fresh water. We must hurry."

Sam grabbed for the bag, and Maria said, "No, leave it. It'll only slow us down."

"I can't, lass. There is enough treasure in jewels and gold to last more than ten lifetimes for both of us."

"You mean for the three of us," she said.

Sam froze and tried to speak, but all he could do was stammer. Maria continued, "You have a son, and his name is Joseph."

He squeezed her around the waist and gave her a quick kiss. "We should make more," he said.

They moved from shadow to shadow and dune to dune as they approached her shack, beyond which was the entrance to the marsh. Suddenly, Sam pointed to the shadowy figure of a man on horseback and Mr. Pratt.

"We know you're out there, you whore. No sooner does some pirate wash up on the beach than you throw yourself at him. Tell us his name so we can put it on his headstone. However, I have a deal. Come forward, and no harm will come to you," said Pratt.

Both Sam and Maria knew he was lying. They hid in the shadows for some time as Pratt peered into the darkness. "We can't stay here. We've got to get around them to the marsh before daybreak. It's our only chance," said Maria.

She chose the best way to the marsh that would keep them in the shadows, but an opening in the clouds exposed light from the moon and dissolved the shadow when they were just yards from the marsh entrance.

"There they are!" shouted Pratt, and he ran toward them with a dagger and pistol in his hands. He lowered the pistol, and Maria could see the barrel pointed at her as Pratt approached within point-blank range. The hammer snapped, and the flint struck steel, but there was no report. The powder was wet from the storm. He continued his rush toward her, but Sam tripped him, and Pratt fell head first, ingesting a mouth full of sand. He got on his hands and knees, choking, and Sam kicked him in the ribs, taking him out of the fight.

Maria screamed, "Watch out, Sam!" as Mr. Ryder galloped toward him, leaning forward in the saddle, the tip of his saber pointing at Sam.

"Run for the marsh!" Sam shouted back. Diablo reared up, flashing his hooves like a war horse. As Sam ducked away from the hooves, he could see that Ryder was holding his saber in his left hand. Ryder slashed at him with a practiced stroke, but Sam held up the bag of treasure to block the blow. He rolled under Diablo, emerging on the other side and grabbing a handful of sand, throwing it in Ryder's face and temporarily blinding him. Sam momentarily dropped the bag, drew his dagger, and slashed Diablo in the hindquarter, causing the stallion to buck and unseat his rider. Sam grabbed the remains of the bag and followed Maria into the marsh. As he did so, two shots rang out. Mr. Ryder stood holding a smoking pistol in each hand.

Pratt approached Mr. Ryder, holding a jeweled necklace and a handful of gold coins that spilled from the bag. "Look at this. The necklace alone is enough to set up a man for life. When it's light, we can search the marsh. With the booty from the wreck and what that witch and her companion have, we'll be rich forever."

"No, that treasure is part of payment due me, and you can't have it," said Ryder as he reloaded his pistols in the leeward side of the shack. "You can have the treasure from the *Whydah,* but I don't think you'll live long enough to enjoy it. You see, you're worse than the pirates you plan to execute. I overheard you planning to have me killed by your accomplices, which is a joke since they don't think I exist. You're too greedy, and you fail to keep your word." He pressed the barrel of one of the pistols against Pratt's chest and pulled the trigger.

The storm raged for three days, after which Pratt's body was found by the townspeople. The priceless necklace was stuffed in his mouth, and the word "Pirate" was carved on his forehead. The people of Chatham guessed that the murder was the work of the witch Maria Hallett and a person or persons unknown. They searched the marsh and found no other treasure nor a trace of Maria and Sam, living or dead. There was also no trace of Bartholomew Ryder.

CHAPTER TWENTY-TWO

I sat in the library, puzzled. That was the end of the book? There was still no indication of a title or who wrote the thing. I knew that Joseph Hallett/ Bellamy and his offspring survived. After all, I was part of his line, but there was no indication of what happened to Sam and Maria or the treasure. The Maria Hallett Marsh was down the road in Wellfleet, and it seemed a good place to visit to get a feel for what they endured. I had to admit that I was obsessed, and I began to wonder if the other Josephs in my line had had the opportunity to read the book and resisted Bartholomew or his ilk, continuing to wind up on the wrong side of the "contract." I knew I was mentally slipping and could easily follow in their footsteps.

My therapist referred me to a psychiatrist. He stroked his beard and said, "Hmm." Then he suggested a cocktail of meds, including mood stabilizers, antipsychotics, and a slew of extras to control the side effects. I took the scripts and threw them away as soon as I got out of his office. I knew what med I needed, and the answer was John Powers. When I arrived at the pub, Riley greeted me and said, "I'd hate to lose you as a customer, but this is your last chance. If I have to put you in a cab this time, it'll be a one-way ride, understand?"

I nodded. "I understand. I'll have a double Powers with rocks on the side." I looked to my right and noticed Bart taking a seat.

"Not in here," I told him. "This is the only place I can regain my sanity now that the wife has removed all the booze from the house, and I don't want to get kicked out."

"We can take a ride in my car," said Bart.

"Thanks, but I'm not ready to ride with the Devil."

"Ha, that's good. Because you already are. That's why you were allowed to read the book. You know, to bring you up to speed as to what you owe."

Having done all the research and read the book, I suspected that Bart might say something similar, and feeling manipulated, I was furious. "Not here and not in your car, asshole. On the bench across the street by the library. All the winos hang out there, so it won't be unusual to see someone talking to themselves."

Instead of the bench by the library, we settled on a secluded dune overlooking the harbor. I looked at Bart and unloaded. "It ends here," I told him. "I ain't playing, and I ain't paying."

Bart produced a paper bag with a bottle of Powers in it, "Don't worry, it's not drugged. It's just good old Irish whiskey." He took a swig.

"That's a joke. I take the word of a devil?" But I took a drink from the bottle.

"Not necessarily a devil. Just someone to collect a debt. You know, all the Joes in your line were just as problematic, and no good came of it. You can opt out, but who knows what would happen. Now, what did you say your son's given name is?"

We were sitting on a bench next to each other, and on impulse, I grabbed Bart by the lapels and threw him to the ground, landing on top of him. I was about to head-butt him when I heard a click and felt the barrel of a gun poking me in the ribs.

"It's real enough, but I think you know that from what happened to Pratt. We're all alone, and it would just look like a suicide. What with the way you've been acting lately, who'd blame you? Then it's on to your son."

"You'd take him anyway, you son of a bitch."

"Ha. Where I come from, that's almost a compliment. We can end it here. It's your choice." He raised an eyebrow.

"So let me get this straight. I sign on the dotted line, and my family is left unmolested, and you get to stick hot pokers up my ass for the remainder of eternity."

"I have to admit that would be amusing, but that's a Christian invention of how things go down, and it still wouldn't pay the debt. Besides, eternity is infinite. Your puny ass simply isn't worth it and would wear out in no time.

You see, things have changed. Your distant relative Black Sam Bellamy, has something I want, and it was in that bag he hauled ashore. Being captain, he took the choicest pieces of loot. Never mind what it's for. I know he had it because it was with the necklace Pratt wound up trying to eat. It's in the marsh."

"So manipulating Maria was just a way of getting Sam back here so you could get your magic potion or whatever."

"No. I often make deals with vulnerable clients because you never know when they'll pay off. I mean, look at the mortgage rates in redlined neighborhoods. Do you think that happens by accident? It's when Sam went pirate and captured the *Whydah,* which had what I wanted on it, that my focus changed."

"Look, I don't know what you want with the marsh. Knowing Maria, they made their way out and probably wound up as Mr. and Mrs. Jones living in the eighteenth-century version of Palm Beach."

"Bartholomew Ryder rarely misses. They didn't make it out of the marsh; they simply weren't found. The place is, after all, called Maria Hallett Marsh."

"Yeah, and the place is several hundred acres. I wouldn't know where to start."

"There's been little rain lately, and it's mostly dry, except over by the spring, which is just a trickle. Here's a map of what the marsh was like back in their day. Study it, and I'll meet you in the parking lot across from the marsh tomorrow before sunrise."

I studied the map, and much had changed over the centuries. Compared with a modern topographical map and a shot from Google Earth, except for where the spring kept the topography reasonably consistent, the shrubs and even the forest that had grown near the marsh had been obliterated by the dunes swallowing them. I knew if I was going to find anything, it wouldn't be on the well-traveled trails.

I had a few things going for me. The first was that it was October, so most of the foliage was off the trees, and the reeds were likely beaten down by an early frost. The fair-weather hikers prevalent in the summer were also gone. So I'd have few curious onlookers to deal with. Second, the map given to me by Bart showed trails not marked on modern surveys.

The weather looked good for the morning, but a northeast blow was forecast for the evening. When I got to the parking lot, Bart was a no-show. Screw him, I'd go on my own, so I took my folding entrenching tool, poncho, and Thermos of coffee out of the trunk. My attempts at navigating the marsh didn't go well. Thanks to low-lying early morning fog, even with a map, compass, and GPS on my cell phone, I quickly got lost. Then, the predicted nor'easter put in an appearance several hours early. Clearly, I lacked the navigation skills of my long-dead ancestor. Even in the depression of the marsh, the wind was screaming, and the rain was horizontal. By noon, it blew close to fifty miles per hour. The sky was dark, and I could hear the thunder of the surf magnified beyond its normal rumble.

Drenched and shivering, I had to find shelter. The ground was too wet to lie down or sit on, and the rain made more puddles as the marsh filled with water. It took hours to get to safety. I walked in a circle, crossing my old tracks. Angry and frustrated, I determined it would be best if I headed for the most reliable landmark by hiking toward the sound of the surf. I reached the edge of the marsh and found some shelter in the crevice between some high dunes. As I surveyed my surroundings, I was reintroduced to a phenomenon I had seen before. Over the years, the dunes had moved and uncovered a landscape of brush and trees that had been buried centuries before. While marginally interesting, the existing terrain didn't provide enough cover, so I broke out my entrenching tool, scraped a hole in the sand, and huddled under my poncho with my coffee.

I was damp and cold, but the coffee gave me energy and helped to warm me, reducing the potential of my falling victim to hypothermia. Unfortunately, the third and last cup did something else, and I had to exit my hole before my bladder burst or I embarrassed myself.

I took aim at the dune across from my ditch. At first, there was a glimmer of something reflecting off my stream in the pale light. Not a big deal, I thought, since there's glass, aluminum cans, and other debris buried in the sand all over the beach and dunes. However, whatever was causing the reflection was attached to a chain, and that chain was made of gold!

I grabbed the entrenching tool and started to scrape, uncovering more jewels and coins along with bits of a rotten canvas bag. After an hour, I had a pile of jewels and gold and silver coins. Then I struck bone, and when I uncovered a skull, I knew the remains were human. The bones were bleached white from being covered and uncovered over the years. At first, I recoiled from the sight, but curiosity got the better of me. As I brushed the sand away, I began to feel like an archeologist on the Discovery Channel.

The sands revealed two skeletons that were entwined. The bigger one had the smaller one spooned within his arms, pulling the smaller one close. I'm no anatomist, but I could see that both had been shot. The bigger one was shot in the upper torso near the shoulder, shattering the scapula where the slug remained, and the smaller one was shot in the left side, fracturing some of the ribs. It took a bit of digging, but I was able to locate the second projectile, which was distorted from the impact. Judging from the bits of clothing and the woman's shoes on the smaller of the skeletons, the remains were colonial, and the slugs I recovered were large caliber rounds and not modern. It all added up. These had to be the remains of my ancestors, Sam Bellamy and Maria Hallett.

I covered them up, leaving a gold chain I found with them. I still don't understand my motivation for doing so. I like to think it was out of respect. Or, considering all the strange things I'd experienced over the past months, it was payment to keep them in their grave. I didn't need a crazed skeleton with a cutlass splitting my head some dark night.

Wrapping the booty in my poncho, I made it into a bundle, and I put the lead balls in my pocket along with two gold sovereigns I found just as I was leaving. I fingered a pretty blue stone that was bigger than a robin's egg, and I put that in the Thermos. A heavy gold cross encrusted with jewels and inscribed with strange writing on the chain also caught my eye. Feeling a bit like a pirate, I put it around my neck.

The wind still howled, but the rain

had been reduced to a few drops that stung when they hit me. I climbed to the top of the dune to get my bearings, and to my surprise, I could see the parking lot. The lights of the cars on Route 6 were about a half mile from where I stood. When I got to the car, I turned the heat up full blast to warm up. I examined the old chart given to me by Bart and estimated where I found the bodies. According to the map, the dunes created a reverse entrance in colonial times that made a hiding place impossible to find if you were unfamiliar with the dunes and marsh. I could only guess that in the couple's last moments, with both of them wounded, Sam had tried to carry Maria to safety. She must have directed them to the spot where they perished and were covered with sand as the storm blew, hiding them until I found them.

A sudden knock on my window

scared the crap out of me because I was so deep in thought. Bart motioned for me to get out of the car. The fact that he held a nickel-plated Colt .45 automatic, pointed straight at me, added to my urgency.

"You didn't wait," he said.

"You were late."

"Did you find anything?"

"Not a thing," I said.

"What's that?" he demanded, poking the cross around my neck with the muzzle of the .45.

"Oh, that's a cross me mother gave to me for me First Communion."

"Don't get smart with me. You're not even Catholic." He poked me in the stomach with the muzzle, doubling me over. "Hand it over."

"Take it," I said.

"Give it to me," he demanded, poking me again.

I had a sudden insight and started

to laugh. "I get it. You can't take it if somebody's wearing it. What is it? This thing has some sort of mumbo-jumbo power. What? I bet I could use it to scare off vampires or get out of jail free."

"Give!" he snarled, poking me again.

"You can beat the crap out of me and even kill me, but I bet you can't touch it until I give it to you freely. I bet while I'm wearing this thing, bullets will just bounce off. Ain't that a bitch."

Bart pushed me back, and I could see from the look in his eyes that I was right. He poked around in my car, found the bundle of booty, and threw it into the Chevelle SS. "Is that all?"

"Well, as much as I could find," I said as I held the cross up in the manner that one would ward off a vampire.

"I'm not a vampire, asshole. They don't exist. Hand it over."

"First, we deal. The contract is terminated, I walk away, and you never come back, ever."

"I could blow your brains out right now," he hissed, leveling the .45.

"Good thinking. You leave a body in a parking lot with a priceless antique cross around its neck. Even if you try to make it look like a suicide, you wouldn't get the cross. Who's the asshole now? I'll make it easy for you. You void the contract, and then you get the cross."

He went to his car, took the book out of the back seat, and dropped it at my feet. "The book's the contract. You can do with it what you like once I get the cross."

"Just one thing: who wrote the manuscript? It's in Maria's blood, but she couldn't have written it. And where'd you get all her blood?"

"Your   reading   comprehension

sucks. She cut her finger when she shook on the contract. As for who wrote the book, get drunk some Samhain, and maybe the curtain will be thin enough for you to find out. Aside from the cross, is that all of it?"

I pretended to think for a moment. "Oh, that's right. I've got two sovereigns and a pair of pistol balls. I'm keeping the pistol balls as family keepsakes and one of the coins for expenses and damages compensating me for mental distress. It wasn't easy bamboozling that poor therapist," I said, flipping him one coin.

"Fair enough. The cross, and then we're done."

"Not quite. Put the gun in your car. You know more people are killed in the US in accidental shootings and suicide than in holdups."

Bart shook his head and threw the gun on the back seat.

I felt more than a little anxiety taking the cross off my neck, but all Bart did was throw it in his backseat with the gun. He burned a long patch of rubber as he left the lot. I watched the Chevy's tail lights get smaller, and I noticed there were no rubber marks where he peeled out. When I picked up the book, it crumbled in my hands, and it had turned to dust by the time I reached my car. Picking up the Thermos, I shook it and heard the rattle of the jewel within. Then I checked my mobile to confirm the GPS locations where I stashed several coins and baubles. I smiled. What did Bartholomew Ryder expect? I'm the direct descendant of a pirate.

AUTHOR'S NOTE

Sometimes inspiration comes from unexpected places. This was the case with *The Strange Story of Maria Hallett*.

While working on a collection of short stories for each month of the year, I went to Cape Cod, Massachusetts, looking for inspiration for an October story. Being an avid sailor and amateur boat builder, and having sailed over the waters of the Cape, I stopped at the *Whydah* Pirate Museum in West Yarmouth. The museum does an excellent job of telling the story of the history and wreck of the *Whydah*, a pirate ship salvaged by Barry Clifford and his team. Connected to the loss of the *Whydah* in the spring of 1717 is a love story about Maria Hallett, a teenage lass living on Cape Cod, and the ship's captain, "Black Sam" Bellamy.

The facts surrounding their relationship are hazy. Sam Bellamy is a documented historical figure and was a very successful pirate until the *Whydah* wrecked on the shoals of the outer Cape. However, the history of Maria Hallett is unclear, and Maria Hallett may not have been her actual name. Legend implies that she gave birth out of wedlock to Sam's child, who may have died in infancy. As a result, she could have been shunned by her community as she waited for Sam's promised return.

One of the characters that elbowed her way into the story was Cape Cod herself. Years ago, as a licensed pilot, I departed Lawrence Municipal Airport on the North Shore of Massachusetts. After flying across Cape Cod Bay and picking up the Provincetown Pilgrim Monument at the bitter end of the Cape under sunny skies, I flew at a low altitude along the Outer Cape. An east wind blew over fifteen knots, and the surf rolled over the sandbars where the *Whydah* had been forced aground over two hundred years before. The chaos caused by the breaking waves was awe-inspiring, even though we observed their action at five hundred feet. I circled a commercial fishing boat beyond the breakers. She rolled significantly in a sea that was building, causing her crew to brace themselves against the ship's motion as they tended their gear. Years later, I thought about the vessel and decided that it may have been the *Vast Explorer*, Barry Clifford's research and salvage vessel. She was in the vicinity of Marconi Beach, near where the wreck was found. Unlike the *Whydah*, they had a trusty diesel and a marine radio, allowing them to work close to the breakers that caused the ship's demise.

We were lucky, too, because we could check the weather at Provincetown Airport by radio. The report was not encouraging: a storm front was roaring in from the Atlantic. We executed the pilot's best friend, a 180-degree turn, as we climbed to three thousand feet.

With the wind to our backs, we scampered back to Lawrence Airport, where we landed, chased by black storm clouds. Quickly we tied the aircraft down, minutes before being engulfed by driving rain and winds gusting over forty miles an hour. This weather event was not forecast on the marine weather radio channel, nor were we briefed about such weather by Flight Service before our departure. The event was a good example of how unpredictable Cape Cod weather can be. She has a mind of her own, and I suspect that at times she has homicidal intentions.

Another character who put in an unexpected appearance was John King. When the ship on which he was a passenger was captured by Sam Bellamy, John, a ten-year-old boy, was offered the choice of remaining with his mother or joining the pirates, and he chose to join the pirates. His reasons are lost to history, but we know he existed because his remains were excavated by Clifford's team when divers found part of a child's skeleton crushed between a cannon and part of the ship's hull on the seafloor.

What a tale John could tell! As a retired child psychologist, I collected as many facts about John King as I could and did my best to create a coherent profile of the lad.

Samhain, the Celtic origin of Halloween, has been a longtime interest of mine. The ancient Celts believed that at certain times of the year, usually at the onset of winter, the veil between the living and the dead was thin enough that a living person could pass through. The prospect of including Samhain and eighteenth-century beliefs about the supernatural, and adding a few villains, the *Whydah*, Sam, and Maria, was too tempting to resist. It created the perfect recipe for a love story and adventure. I threw these characters, beliefs, and events in a batter and stirred.

The character's behaviors are speculation, but being a sailor, I tried to make the description of the *Whydah's* demise as accurate as possible, based on contemporary reports, my own experience, and archeological evidence uncovered by Barry Clifford's salvage team.

I hope this story captures your interest and that you consider visiting the Pirate Museum. But there are more places hidden around the Cape that are fun to visit if you know where to look. For example, Marconi Beach not only has remnants of the old Marconi radio tower but is surrounded by high dunes reaching the surf below. If you stand on them and look out into the Atlantic, you can feel some of the emotions Maria may have felt as she waited for Sam's return and witnessed the *Whydah* breaking up, or experience what Joe felt when he wandered the dunes looking for Sam's treasure. If you are lucky enough to go during the summer, you might catch a glimpse of one of Barry Clifford's research vessels excavating for more artifacts just offshore.

But more waits behind the dunes in the White Cedar Swamp, which, legend has it, used to be called Maria Hallett Swamp. The National Park Service has constructed an easy-to-follow trail.

However, be mindful of the forecast and the time of day. When the weather is overcast, the swamp can feel foreboding, and if the trail markers are not visible, it would be easy to become disoriented and lost like the characters in the story. I bet it would be even creepier to visit around Halloween—oops, I mean Samhain—when the veil between the living and the dead is thinnest.

On second thought, I'll pass. I'm not sure I want to shake hands with a long-dead pirate.

—R.Z.

ACKNOWLEDGMENTS

I wrote *The Strange Story of Maria Hallett* with considerable help. Barry Clifford's book *Expedition Whydah* was one of the sources that inspired me to write the story. His book is chock full of facts about the history of the wreck, as well as descriptions of the artifacts he recovered. I received guidance from my daughter, Marlena Zapf, a professional editor, and I attended workshops at GrubStreet Center for Creative Writing in Boston. Both aided in sharpening my writing skills. Some of the most important help came from my writing coach, Janet Young, who has been instrumental in encouraging my work. Others who have supported my writing include my wife, Nancy, and the crew at WHAV

97.9 FM in Haverhill, Massachusetts, which broadcasts my short stories once a month, as read by Win Damon and Jenifer Cosgrove. Feedback from early readers of *Maria Hallett,* including Doug Teague and George Skelly, provided invaluable advice.

Richard Zapf is a retired clinical neuropsychologist whose stories explore adventure, love, loss, and the human condition. A longtime sailor, boat builder, and licensed pilot, he has extensive knowledge of the waters around Cape Cod.